THE TRAP IS SPRUNG!

It started when Bill noticed a nut-brown face that instantly stood out from the crowd—a stoic, unreadable face with black eyes sunk deep behind prominent cheekbones. The shako hat with its leather chin strap looked South American, Argentina maybe.

Their gazes collided for a moment; then the man's eyes slid away from him. He carried a Smith & Wesson tucked behind his sash, the special-issue, two-and-a-half-pound revolver sold to the Czar's government in Russia. Bill recognized the extra finger grip on the trigger guard.

The man passed by, and Wild Bill kept a close eye on him. Too late, he realized that was his big mistake. The hard case was only a diversion—by the time Hickok saw the second man lunge at him, it was too late to react.

WILD BILL

POINT RIDER

JUDD COLE

LEISURE BOOKS NEW YORK CITY

Fondly dedicated to "Pop-a-top" Charlie Waites,
who still owes me $20.

A LEISURE BOOK®

January 2001

Published by

Dorchester Publishing Co., Inc.
276 Fifth Avenue
New York, NY 10001

ISBN 0-8439-4823-X

Visit us on the web at www.dorchesterpub.com.

POINT RIDER

Chapter One

"It ain't death I fear, Wild Bill," remarked "Gentleman John" Haskins to J. B. Hickok after nearly two hours of dead silence.

Hickok, busy studying the creosote scrubland just north of Del Rio, Texas, slewed around in the saddle to look at his prisoner.

"No, sir, it's knowing *exactly when* death is coming, Bill, that's the part I can't abide," Haskins assured him in his amiable Tennessee twang. "Out here a man expects death at any time. But a hanging date—now see, that gives you time to count down to your own dying. There, sir, is what I fear."

Hickok, a neckerchief pulled over the lower half of his face to cut the thick trail dust, nodded to concede the point.

"All you had to do, Johnny, was push me to a gunfight and be done with it. You or me. You're the one tossed down your shooter; hell, I can't shoot an unarmed man."

Gentleman John snorted. "Why not? There wasn't much else you *didn't* shoot."

Armed with a half-dozen John Doe warrants, and more guts than good sense, Hickok had entered Rustler's Roost, up on the Concho River, in a blaze of gunfire. When Gentleman John saw three of his toughest men shot to rag tatters, he got snow in his boots and surrendered. Thus had crumbled the largest rustling ring in South Texas.

Wild Bill knew, however, that it didn't end with that scrape up on the Concho. He expected more trouble, and at any time now. Gentleman John was the big he-dog among hard-tails in the Live Oak country, and he'd never go to the gallows without a fox play or two.

"Bill," Gentleman John said perhaps a half-mile later, "my mouth feels stuffed with cotton. I'd be beholden for a sup of something wet. Some libation with kick being preferred."

Hickok reined in his strawberry roan, letting his prisoner's horse catch up. A long lead line connected the other horse to Bill's bridle ring. Haskins's hands were tied behind his back with strong cord that bit deeper the more a prisoner struggled against it. Only his stirruped feet held him in the saddle.

Hickok shook open the long gray duster that did double duty: It protected his dark twill suit while also hiding the two ivory-gripped Colt Model P six-shooters that had become his trademark all over the frontier.

By habit he loosened both weapons in their holsters, minimizing friction drag if he needed them quick. Then he produced a signed bottle of Old Taylor bourbon from his coat pocket. Gentleman John's coarse-grained face eased into an ear-to-ear smile. But despite that pleasant smile and his impeccable manners, his eyes were as hard as his muscles.

Bill carefully poured a generous snort into Haskins's mouth. The rustler king smacked his lips appreciatively.

"Now, that's the boy you don't want to give the slip to! I thank you, sir. Colonel Taylor's fermentations are unmatched anywhere."

"Anything else," Bill agreed amiably, "is burro piss. Now let's make tracks, old son. I plan to reach Del Rio before sunset. I've grown soft since our war days, Johnny. I require sheets, a hot bath, the comforts of a woman, and a good poker game."

"Now, Bill, if comfort is your boy, why in Sam Hill would you pick Del Rio? You'd ought to've turned me in over at San Antone. That place is settling up, by the Lord Harry. Del Rio is just a bordertown roach pit."

Hickok needed no such reminder. He presently had a decent hotel room going to waste in San Antonio. Despite being so tired he could feel the dragging weight of the cartridges in his shell belt, he had been forced to pass his room by and bear due west to Del Rio instead.

"This trip's your fault, not mine," Hickok reminded him. "To you a cow's a cow, and you're indifferent to where you steal it."

"Steal is a damned ugly word, Bill. I prefer to call it 'rescuing mavericks.' "

Bill snorted, the sound making his horse, Fireaway, prick his ears. In truth, the infamous Gentleman John Haskins specialized in "slicing off some beef" from massive drives pushing up the Chisholm Trail toward shipping points like Ellsworth and Abilene. He and his men were experts at employing running irons to cleverly alter established brands right alongside the trail.

"Uh-huh, well, when you rescue a cow in Texas, then sell it in Kansas," Bill informed him dryly, "that's a federal crime. So I have to book you into the U.S. Marshals at Del Rio."

Bill opened his canteen and splashed water on his face, then Gentleman John's. They had both slept in the open the night before, curling behind meager windbreaks of sage brush. This final expanse, between the Nueces River and Del Rio, was a God-forgotten desert of bone-dry washes and salt sage.

"There's Del Rio," Wild Bill announced as they crested a redrock bluff overlooking the muddy brown meanders of the Rio Grande—or the Rio Bravo to those who lived south of it.

"Just in time, too," Hickok added, looking overhead as heat lightning exploded like muzzle flashes behind the clouds. "Looks like a gully-washer making up."

"Well, then, sir," Gentleman John said, his tone quietly resigned. "If the great farce is finally over, so be it! John Haskins played his part well, and now he's weary of it. Besides, how many men get to be escorted to the hangman by Wild Bill Hickok? Hey? It's been an honor, sir, and no hard feelings."

Hickok was not fooled for one second by this rhetorical smoke. Give Haskins a moment's opportunity, and he'd run like a river when the snow melts.

Bill dallied the lead line around his saddle horn, shortening it for this final approach into town. Even Del Rio, Bill noticed, had grown rapidly since the War Between the States.

First came the abandoned buildings at the edge of town, choked with tumbleweed and Russian thistle. Hickok's eyes remained in constant motion. Fire-away could feel his master's caution—the gelding, too, brought his head up, ears pricked forward, as they advanced along wide, wagon-rutted Main Street.

Next came the dugouts and sheds of the dirt-poor Mexicans, Indians, and 'breeds, a sleepy section that would come alive after sundown. They trotted past a dance hall that had seen so many fights the windows were boarded up. Past the livery barn, where a handsome dun horse was enjoying a good roll in manure.

The center of town was much more active and crowded. Cowboys wearing bandannas and leather chaps lounged everywhere, sun-crimped eyes watching the new arrivals with bored curiosity.

The adobe courthouse hove into view ahead, plastered white and topped with red tiles. But even now, this close, Hickok did not let down his guard. The stories about Gentleman John and his loyal minions were more than backcountry lore and saloon gossip.

"End of the line, *compadre*," Haskins said quietly as Bill reined in at the courthouse.

Hickok didn't like the ambiguity of the remark. The end of whose line? He brought his right foot out of the stirrup and swung down, landing light as a cat in the street. He looped his reins around the tie rail, eyes scanning everyone who passed.

Like most survivors on the American frontier, Hickok had learned to tell a man's home range by his rig and the way he shaped his hat. Men from northern ranges, for example, preferred a low, crimped crown, while on the southern ranges a higher, rounded crown was more common.

As he helped Haskins to the ground, Wild Bill carefully gauged the home range and profession of every man who thumped by on the weather-rawed boardwalk. And good thing, for when the expected trouble came, it happened the way trouble usually happened out west. It was sudden, violent, and brief.

It started when Bill noticed a nut-brown face that instantly stood out from the crowd—a stoic, unreadable face with black eyes sunk deep behind prominent cheekbones. The shako hat with its leather chin strap looked South American, Argentina maybe.

Their gazes collided for a moment, then the man's eyes slid away from his. He carried a Smith & Wesson tucked behind his sash, the special-issue, two-and-a-half-pound revolver sold to the Czar's government in Russia. Bill recognized the extra finger grip on the trigger guard.

The man passed by, and Wild Bill kept a close eye on him. Too late, he realized that was his big mistake. The hardcase was only a diversion—by the time Hickok saw the second man lunge at him, it was too late to react.

Wild Bill took a hard, straight punch right in the wind, and his knees started to buckle. Luckily his enemies hoped to avoid the sound of gunfire right out front of the courthouse. A knife blade flashed fire in the sun as the attacker made a vicious and deliberate swipe at the inside of Bill's right elbow.

Lightning reflexes let Bill pull his arm back just in time, so only his duster and coat sleeve were sliced open. Clearly the attacker was a blade expert—he was trying to sever the tendon inside the elbow. That was the quickest and easiest way to render an arm useless for life, since tendons could not knit or heal.

"Hijo!" the attacker cursed when Wild Bill drilled two bullet holes into his heart, dropping him like a sack of grain. The man on the boardwalk whirled, making a stab for iron, but Hickok

13

pivoted half-right on one heel and killed him with one clean shot to the brain.

"Aww, damnit, Bill," Gentleman John whined, his tone squeaky with disappointment. "You just put the kabosh on Rico Aragon and 'Braska Newcomb, my top hands. This child really *is* going to dance on air."

"Better you than me," Bill remarked calmly. "It's all right, Jude," he called out. A whey-faced jailer clutching a shotgun had peeked outside to see what the racket was. "I just plugged two of Gentleman John's associates. They won't be needing a doctor, just the undertaker."

Bill's first, reflexive action was to thumb reloads into his gun. Eyes still sweeping to all sides, he turned Haskins over to the jailer, then collected his mileage pay from the disburser upstairs. Any federal warrant paid a penny a mile to the arresting officer.

Hickok collected a little over three dollars for Haskins—no Rockefeller fortune, he figured, but added on top of the four dollars a day Allan Pinkerton paid him, it was a nice little bonus. It meant he could play a little poker later, maybe even win enough to tell Pinkerton *adios* for a while.

Right now, though, all he required was a hot bath, a thick steak, and a feather-stuffed mattress for his aching bones. Then he would make the return ride to San Antonio and that Judas-haired beauty who sang at the Lone Star Saloon.

He descended the brick steps of the courthouse,

gazing at his knife-shredded sleeve. A shudder moved down his spine as he realized how close that blade had come to giving him a dead arm.

"Old son," he muttered to himself, "that one was close, and they're shaving closer every time. Pinkerton has got desk jobs, too. Maybe it's time to ask for one."

"Confound the damn thing anyway!" Joshua Robinson swore out loud.

Strong language for this son of Quakers, and the cause of it was a bulky new contraption that must have been invented in hell to drive mortals mad. Called a typewriter, it sat atop the writing desk before him.

Allan Pinkerton had recently delivered it, in person, from his new branch office here in San Antonio. The famous detective had raved about the device, how it would transform world culture or some such truck.

So far, though, Josh had spent most of his time untangling knotted ribbons and separating jammed keys.

This newfangled contraption would never catch on, he told himself again. Not without plenty of changes. Why, it had nothing but capital letters! And no semicolon, nor even a numeral one!

Someone rapped on the door of his hotel room, and Josh instantly welcomed any excuse to cut short his typing practice.

"Open!" he called out.

"Joshua, how fares it with the typing, laddie-buck?"

A tall, slightly paunchy man wearing bushy burnsides and a smoke-gray wool suit strolled in, his manner brisk and businesslike. A Scottish brogue was evident in his trilled *r*'s and elongated vowels.

"Mr. Pinkerton, how are you, sir? To be honest, this game is not worth the candle. Why, a fellow can't even read what he's typed unless he takes the paper out. And the letters are arranged alphabetically, but that's just thickheaded. They should be set up so the most frequently used letters are right under your fingers or close to 'em. Sort of a home row, just like they're arranged in a printer's galley."

"A home row, eh?"

Beaming, Pinkerton pulled a flipback pad and a stub of pencil from his pocket, making quick notes.

"*That's* the gait, Joshua! That's why I brought you one. I know Chris Sholes, the inventor. It's only been in production a few years now—it's still being improved. Soon, it will be selling like buckwheat cakes."

Josh knew Pinkerton was a great enthusiast of things modern. The wily old Scotsman also tended to support new inventions with sizable investments, and thus he had become a master at a fairly new American creation some called "promotion," others "hucksterism."

"If you came to see Wild Bill," Josh added, "you

won't find him in his room. He rode up to the Concho river last week, looking for Gentleman John Haskins."

A sly look crossed Pinkerton's face, and he closed the door with his heel.

"You're behind times. That job's closed out," Pinkerton informed him. "Jamie wired from Del Rio this morning. Haskins is locked down tight, and Jamie should be back in San Antonio in a few days."

"Jamie" was Hickok, whom he had known since before the war and had always refused to call Wild Bill.

Josh's eyes widened at the news. "Man alive! Is this an exclusive, Mr. Pinkerton?"

The sly glint was back in the detective's eyes. "Come now, lad. We're fellow professionals, both of us free, white, and twenty-one. Call me Allan."

"Yessir, Mr.—uh, Allan. But I'm only twenty."

"No one's counting out west. Yes, it's an exclusive."

Josh immediately stood up and, straining at the weight, put the typewriter back in its crate beside the desk. Haskins locked down! Jiminy! Not only the most notorious rustler in Longhorn country, but wanted for twelve killings and wartime desertion. He had been made even more notorious by consecutive write-ups in the nationally read *Police Gazette*.

"There's at least three other reporters camped in town these days," Josh told the older man. "All trying to be first to get the latest 'Wild West' stories onto the wire. And Wild Bill stories are top of the line. So, thanks."

Pinkerton nodded. "Most journalists would kiss the devil's ass for what I just gave you. But you stand out from the pack, Joshua. I, too, must thank you."

Pinkerton pulled a cushioned footrest close to Josh's chair and sat down.

"Son, does it not occur to you that I've come to see *you*, not your famous mentor? And I maun also be wonderin'—is Hickok the only famous chap currently residing here at the Cattleman's Palace?"

Josh shook his head. "You're too far north for me, sir—uh, Allan."

"Why, I mean *you*, lad! Any civilized person in America knows the *New York Herald* is the greatest newspaper in the nation. But let's not be falsely modest, Joshua. Its circulation has almost doubled since you became far-west correspondent."

Josh felt himself swell with pride. Well, wasn't it all true? Never mind if the new ladies' fashions section had something to do with it, too.

"Now, don't take me wrong," Pinkerton assured him. "J. B. Hickok is truly an extraordinary man. Personally, I think only Daniel Boone, Jim Bridger, and Kit Carson will stand in American history as his equals at frontier survival. And *no* one is his equal at the quick draw, with the possible exception of Wes Hardin."

Pinkerton, a master at pulpit speech, paused to give his next point extra import.

"But, Joshua, how does the *entire world* know what Hickok's closest friends have learned from observation? I tell you, lad, it's all because of two extraordinary writers: Ned Buntline, novelist, and Joshua Robinson, correspondent."

Even as he oozed these words of praise, Pinkerton slid an envelope from the breast pocket of his coat. Josh glimpsed the official seal of the U.S. War Department in one corner.

"Joshua, an extraordinary and dramatic chapter in American history is now unfolding up north in the South Platte country of Nebraska. Do you know who General Jeremy Schuster is?"

Josh nodded. It was his job to know such things. Schuster was known as Old Sobersides to his men, for the strict Methodist had never been seen to smile or laugh.

"Schuster's commander of the Department of the Dakotas, which is mainly Sixth Cavalry troops."

"Precisely."

Pinkerton handed the youth the letter.

"A stern, sometimes petty, but effective and fair officer. Takes his duties very seriously. Read that, lad."

Josh did. As he progressed, his reporter's instincts became alert like hounds on point.

Dear Mr. Pinkerton,
   The U.S. Army requires your agency's assis-

*tance in a matter of grave importance. Or more
accurately: the services of just one of your op-
eratives, J. B. "Wild Bill" Hickok.*

*A precarious situation exists regarding the
Sioux Indian tribe under Chief White Bear, all
officially wards of the U.S. Government since
they live on the reservation near Ogallala. Repeated raids, presumably by renegades who
have jumped the reservation, have cut off almost all food supplies to the Sioux.*

*As you know, they are forbidden by treaty
from hunting. But most food crops planted by
the Indians have been deliberately destroyed.
Fish streams and game watering holes have
been poisoned, and the few remaining buffalo
this far north have been slaughtered or driven
south. Making a bad situation even worse, I
have just learned that Chief White Bear has
been murdered.*

At this news Josh looked up, his beardless face
astonished.

"Why, I *knew* Chief White Bear! It was his tribe
that Wild Bill and Professor Vogel saved from
mountain fever with Vogel's ice machine."

"I remember," Pinkerton said coyly. "Oh, I remember, Joshua. You had every literate man,
woman, and child in America on tenterhooks
waiting to read how that one turned out."

Josh returned to Old Sobersides's letter.

*In light of this dire situation, the Army has re-
ceived an unusual command. We are ordered*

to procure 1,000 head of good butcher beef and see that it gets up north to the starving Sioux. Since trouble is expected, the drovers will not be cowboys per se, but well-armed enlisted soldiers with experience handling cattle.

I consider it imperative that Hickok serve as point man for this mission of mercy. Based on my at times spotty intelligence reports, the dangers are considerable. I relied on Hickok's vital reconnaissance at Antietam Creek during the Great Rebellion. This man has protected U.S. mail, stagecoaches, freight wagons, and railroad crews. He's also the only sheriff who ever managed to clean up Abilene, Kansas, albeit only temporarily.

Upon receiving a favorable response from you, Allan (please use the telegraph, as time is urgent), a detail of ten soldiers, under the command of Lieutenant Matt Carlson, will be immediately detached for special duty from Fort Trinity to San Antonio.

The Sioux have ample reasons, some fantastic, others real, for mistrusting white men. But Wild Bill is a hero to them. Their plight, I repeat, is dire. I hope to tell them, very soon, that the Ice Shaman is returning to save them.

On behalf of the Army and the American Government, I thank you for your urgent attention to this matter.

Josh handed the letter back. "Schuster mentions renegades who've jumped the rez," the reporter said, a skeptical dimple appearing at the corner of his mouth. "Is he sure renegades have done all these things he's mentioned? I mean, it doesn't make sense they'd poison *Indian* water holes. And where did they get poison?"

Pinkerton spread his hands in a gesture of Gallic diplomacy. "I think the general understands, without stating as much, that somebody besides the Sioux is causing the trouble. That's why he needs Jamie on this drive."

"I don't know," Josh said doubtfully. "I mean, the Sioux are in a dirty corner, all right, and it's a crying shame. But Wild Bill riding point for a cattle drive? I've been sidekicking with Bill over a year now—he's not so fond of the saddle anymore."

Pinkerton conceded this with a nod. "Danger doesn't bother Hickok nearly so much as hard work."

"Yeah, and punching cattle is hard work. So I wouldn't get too set on him for this job."

"Oh, I've already wired Schuster. I told him Hickok will definitely take the assignment."

Josh winced. "What, you mean before you talked it out with Bill?"

"Son, time is nipping at our sitters! I took the liberty of speaking for Jamie. Those soldiers are on their way here. But I want you to think carefully about all this, Joshua. Think like a newspaperman, understand?"

Josh did. And he grasped instantly what Pinkerton was up to—promotion. He wanted the weight of the *New York Herald* behind this one.

"Bill saved this tribe once before," the youth pointed out. "And when he did, it got more ink than anything since Charles Dickens visited America."

"Yes, and that one incident," Pinkerton confessed, "sold the 'detective' to Americans. I opened three branch offices to handle all the cases I received."

"So if Wild Bill could save the same tribe once again, the story would be even bigger." Josh marveled as Pinkerton's thinking became his own.

Pinkerton beamed at the kid's growing enthusiasm. One of the best writers in America was about to take the hook.

"Joshua, the American people love a winner because they are staunch optimists. Absurdly so, at times. Why, I was there when the First New York Regiment marched off for Bull Run. My hand to God, they wore uniforms from Brooks Brothers and carried sandwiches from Delmonico's! We know how their 'two-day war' turned out, don't we? All the more reason to adore Hickok—he's the quintessential American *winner*."

The wily detective-turned-entrepreneur paused, altering his tone slightly.

"But Joshua, as you just mentioned—*you* aren't the only scribb—ahh, I mean writer eager for exclusives on Hickok. I won't be able to sit on this much longer."

Josh didn't need a map to see where Pinkerton was going. This story had all the elements of a true

Western saga: cowboys, Indians, bad guys, and Wild Bill Hickok, an international hero. Whoever first filed this one would get credit for breaking one of the biggest stories since Custer's Seventh was rubbed out.

"One thing I know about Jamie," the detective added with a confident nod, "is how much he eats up the attention. He understands the vital link between the printing press and his 'legend.' "

Pinkerton donned his derby hat and gave Joshua a hearty handshake.

"Remember, laddiebuck, the early bird gets the worm. And no man in America has told the saga of the sagebrush heartland better than you. This story *belongs* to you—don't let some other jasper beat you to it."

On this flattering note, Pinkerton made his exit. Joshua debated for only a few minutes.

"I'll *do* it," he muttered aloud, "and I'll deal with Bill later."

Joshua opened his ink bottle, dipped a steel nib into it, and unwittingly began creating what would soon become Bill Hickok's worst nightmare.

Chapter Two

"Boys," said Harding Ott, looking around at three of his subordinates, "everybody talks about the weather, but nobody does anything about it. You ever notice that?"

None of the men drinking whiskey at the oilcloth-covered table had a response, at first, for this odd remark. The two white men were brothers, Jip and Olney Lucas. The third was a full-blooded Hunkpapa Sioux called Bobcat.

"What's your drift, boss?" Olney finally asked. "You settin' up to be rainmaker now?"

Olney and Jip laughed, and seeing them, Bobcat joined in. His English, which was limited, became almost useless once he started drinking strong water.

Ott was not the least offended by their taunts. He was a big man, better than six feet and carved from granite, hatchet-faced, with shrewd, hard eyes the color of blood onyx.

"No," he replied mildly, pouring himself another jolt of forty-rod. "I'm setting up to be a *town* maker. My drift is quite simple, gents. Big ideas, and big talkers, are a penny the dozen. But I'm the kind of man who gets ten miles down the road before most men can even decide when to leave."

Ott banged the empty bottle on the table a few times. A beautiful Crow Indian woman—still quite young, but already showing hard treatment—stepped past the ratty chenille curtain separating this room from a little slope-off kitchen. The house was cottonwood logs chinked with mud, so crude that nearly transparent animal hides were stretched over the windows in place of glass.

"Woman Dress," Ott called out, wagging the bottle at her, "more whiskey."

She nodded and hurried to take the bottle from him, going outside to the cellar to fill it from the big barrel of wagon-yard whiskey he kept there.

Olney kept his glassy-eyed gaze on the woman until she was gone. Both of the Lucas brothers were towheads, but that was where the resemblance ended. Olney, the youngest, was small-framed, wiry, and lithe, with good looks and the cocky swagger of a natural-born killer. He wore two Colt Lightnings tied low, the inside of his holsters lightly oiled for an effortless draw.

Jip, in contrast, was middle-sized and quite ordinary, with dull eyes and a weak chin in a completely unremarkable face. He was one of those men who "run to type," and thus could easily mingle unnoticed in any crowd. That was handy, especially since he knew how to kill a man six ways to Sunday without ever firing a gun.

"That squaw of yours puts out good grub," Olney told his boss. "She put out anything else that's good?"

Jip sniggered again, and Bobcat dutifully chimed in. The Sioux had been named for the deep red scars, inflicted by a puma, that ran from his left ear to the point of his chin. His mouth, too, was a mean gash in a face ugly as proud flesh.

Harding shrugged indifferently. "All cats look alike in the dark."

"I only take ugly women in the dark," Olney assured him. "Not when they're peart as Woman Dress."

"I'll tell you what, Olney," Harding offered in affable tones. "You boys manage to do a little job for me, and besides the usual eight bits a day, you can have Woman Dress all you want. You too, Jip. She'll do anything I tell her. She has to—I paid her clan a good price to own her."

The Lucas boys exchanged a long glance.

"Boss," Olney assured him, "them's interestin' wages, all right. What's the game?"

"Money, boys. Mammon. Legem pone. I heard a stump-screaming politician call these Great Plains 'the broad front door of the westward movement.' Well, by God, I'm *opening* that door. I sought my fortune beyond the hundredth meridian, and now I'm finally about to hit pay dirt. So all in all, this is a damn good time for you fellows to hitch your wagons to my star."

Jip and Olney exchanged a bemused glance.

"Boss, did you kiss the Blarney Stone?" Olney asked. "You sent word you had a business proposition for us, not a buncha damned peyote talk."

Woman Dress returned and filled all their glasses, then set the bottle near Ott. The moment this was done, she sat on a low, cowhide-covered stool in the back corner; she began grinding wheat in a hand gristmill. Not once did she look at any of the men.

"Hey, Woman Dress," Olney called over. "You like being topped by a white man? Are we better 'n 'em red bucks, hanh?"

"What I hear," Jip tossed in, "is how Injuns ain't got no hair down there. That true, boss?"

Ott just laughed and shook his head.

"You two do beat all," he reprimanded them good-naturedly. "Did you ride thirty miles to ask me that?"

"Hell no," Olney said. "Let's get down to cases."

"Now you're whistling! All three of you know I'm currently attempting to, ahh, shift some Indians to a new position south of the Platte River. They'd still be on their reservation, just another part of it."

He didn't need to add what all three of them already knew: The part he was "shifting" them to was the worthless part of the reservation. Mineral-poor, sandy soil good for nothing but weeds and johnsongrass, better known as locoweed. No trees

for windbreaks from the blowing grit, and no water—not even a rain cistern—for miles around
them.

In contrast, the area presently occupied by the
Sioux was perfectly located for Ott's needs. It was
a huge swath of land between the Kansas Pacific
Railroad and the Colorado border. A little too dry
for dependable crops, it was excellent grazeland if
a man had big acreage, for the grass was good but
somewhat sparse.

"This land I'm trying to free up," Ott told them,
"could easily be irrigated. These Indian farmers
are just primitive dirt-scratchers growing piddlin'
kitchen truck. White men with science could fetch
forty bushels of wheat an acre off that land some-
day."

"You bet your bucket!" Bobcat suddenly spoke
up, so drunk by now he was simply spouting English phrases. The other three men laughed at
him.

"Drink up, Bobcat," Olney encouraged him, fill-
ing his glass again. Few things were more entertaining than Injuns drunk on their asses.

"Problem is," Ott went on, "I've received some
information from a soldier I know at Fort Platte.
He claims there's a cattle drive making up right
now in Texas. The Army evidently plans to point
some beeves north—beeves meant to feed the
Sioux."

Ott topped off Bobcat's glass with more coffin
varnish. The Sioux was in charge of the twenty-
man reservation police force, and somewhat di-

vided in his loyalties—but only when sober. Ott knew the drunker he got, the "whiter" he got.

"Feed the Sioux?" Olney repeated, a smirk easing his lips apart. "Why? Are the Noble Red Men hungry?"

All three white men laughed again, and Bobcat joined in only a few beats late, so inebriated by now his eyes were glass buttons.

In fact, Ott, the Lucas brothers, and the well-bribed Sioux policemen had all joined forces in an effort to drive the tribe south of the Platte. They had robbed shipments of government rations, deliberately destroyed crops, and poisoned any game the Indians might illegally hunt. Ott had even personally killed Chief White Bear and replaced him with a puppet leader named Chinook.

"By now," Ott told the others, "the Sioux headmen are finally talking about moving. They've got no choice—most of the tribe are so hungry they're eating their dogs and the tar paper off the reservation school."

Ott's face took on a granite edge. "But if that beef gets through, boys, we'll be right back where we were—running hard just to stand still."

Only now did the full extent of Ott's meaning—and his dogged determination—show in his voice. Right now Commerce Bluffs—his name for the thriving community that would soon replace the scattered Sioux lodges—existed only in an illegal contract with foreign investors.

But nearby Ogallala, too, had been nothing but a tent town beside the Union Pacific Railroad two short years ago. Now they were putting down boardwalks and electing a mayor. Commerce Bluffs, too, could be built up in jig time—especially with rich foreigners champing at the bit to get even richer in America.

"I want that trail drive headed off," Ott told the Lucas boys. "One way or the other. It's just a handful of soldiers, and that's a long drive. If it's necessary, you can draft a few of Bobcat's rez policemen to help you."

Hearing his name, Bobcat giggled drunkenly. "Kiss my ass, Cochise!" he called out, and the three whites laughed as if it was a capital joke.

But then the mirth just suddenly bled from Ott's hard eyes.

"I don't care if those cows are rustled, shot, poisoned, or just scattered onto free range," he told his toadies. "Anything, just so they don't get through to the tribe. I want those damned redskins relocated by the first frost. I've got investors to pacify and a town to build!"

On the fourth morning after he rode out of Del Rio, Hickok was wide awake and smoking the day's first cheroot. He watched the sun edge over the eastern horizon, still dull and rosy.

He tapped the cigar out on his boot heel, then dropped the butt in his vest pocket to smoke later. He rolled up his blanket and groundsheet, then gathered some gnarled mesquite wood to build a cook fire. He fixed a good meal of bacon and pan bread, washing it down with strong black coffee.

31

While he drank the last of the coffee, taking his time, he made sure to keep his back to a wide cottonwood tree. He had made camp in a little hollow beside a creek, a spot where he could see anyone approaching from any direction.

Fire-away, grazing on a long tether behind him, trotted over when he saw Bill stirring. The strawberry roan nuzzled his shoulder, then snorted a complaint.

"I know, boy," Hickok told the horse, scratching his withers good. "This wiry palomilla grass is poor shakes as fodder. But we'll make San Antone by noon. I promise—after today, it's corn and oats and plenty of rest for you."

At these words, a smile pulled at Bill's lips. Plenty of rest for *both* of us, he vowed. Bill had been invited into a high-stakes poker game in Del Rio, and the luck of the Irish was on him. Now sixty dollars in gold and silver coins bulged the breast pocket of his coat, burning a hole.

Pinkerton could go piss up a rope for all Bill cared. He was sore and saddle-weary, his tailbone aching from damn near two weeks of steady riding. He was taking a few well-deserved weeks off before he accepted another case.

Hickok broke camp, rigged his gelding, then quickly washed up at the creek, making sure to carefully comb out his long blond mustache. While he did this, he was careful not to stand too long in one spot, and he always tried to keep his back covered.

By now it was general knowledge that the man

who delivered Hickok's head to a wealthy Texan named Linton Lofley would earn $10,000. While sheriff of Abilene, Kansas, Hickok had killed Lofley's son Harlan in a fair fight.

But Dame Rumor claimed it was cold-blooded murder—and Hickok was the first to admit that he *had* done some frosty killing in his time. He had survived this long by religiously adhering to one rule: Shoot first, ask questions later. That reputation made him a common murderer in old man Lofley's eyes.

Hickok buckled on his heavy shell belt, sliding the riding thongs around the ivory butts of his .44s. Then he swung up into leather, stabbed both feet into the stirrups, and started Fire-away due east with a squeeze of his knees. He usually let his horse set its own pace, and the roan soon settled into an easy lope.

The terrain in this stretch of south Texas alternated between sagebrush grass and salt-desert shrubs. Turkey buzzards wheeled in the cloudless sky, keeping an expectant eye on him as the next potential feast.

Bill reined in now and then, in stretches of better graze, so Fire-away could take off some grass.

Several times, in the driest stretch just before San Antonio, Hickok spotted piles of bleaching bones—and twice he recognized them as human. When he finally forded the big creek called the San Antonio River, he rode wide past some sandbar willows, fearing ambush.

Finally, however, he arrived safely on the outskirts of town. Hickok pulled his flat, broad-brimmed black hat lower, casting his face in shadow. He also made sure his duster covered both guns. Nonetheless, the town loafers recognized him by his horse and called out greetings to the famous man.

"Hey, Bill! Touch you for luck?"

"Wild Bill! You ever gonna have a showdown with Wes Hardin? He's fast with both hands—your left is slow!"

"Hey, Hickok? How many curly-haired bastards have you sired?"

He bore all of it in stoic silence, gunmetal eyes sweeping left and right as he bore toward the livery stable at the opposite end of town.

I been damn lucky, Bill thought. Two months now in San Antone, and Calamity Jane hasn't sniffed me out—knock on wood, he added as he superstitiously rapped his knuckles against the walnut stock of the Winchester '72 protruding from his saddle scabbard.

Billed reined in at the livery and stripped the rigging from his horse. After currycombing the dried sweat off the roan, he turned it into the paddock and used a scoop to fill the grain trough.

Bill lugged his rig into the tack room and tossed it onto an empty saddlerack. He hung the bridle from a nail, then paused at the long trough out front to rinse the top layer of trail dust off.

Little was on his mind right now except a hot bath, a steak, a bottle of Old Taylor, and a set of clean sheets. He meant to sleep like a winter bear, then maybe look up Ida Gipson, that little redhead at the Lone Star Saloon.

Bill's heels thumped on the boardwalk as he aimed toward the Cattleman's Palace Hotel in the middle of town. When men passed him, he kept his eyes on their hands. Every plate-glass window became a mirror he used to watch the bustling street.

Up ahead, sheltering in the shade of the green awning above Morgan's Mercantile Store, a newsboy was hawking the bulldog edition of the *San Antonio Sentry*.

Wild Bill hadn't caught up on the news for weeks now. He fished in his front pocket for a dime.

"Exter! Exter!" the kid barked in a voice cracking with adolescence. "Read all about it, folks! Ter-r-r-*iff*-ic sensation! Can Wild Bill do it again? Ter-r-r-*iff*-ic sensation, read all about it!"

What in Sam Hill? Hickok wondered. Can I do *what* again? He was used to being written about, but lately he'd been running all over Robin Hood's barn, chasing down rustlers. He hadn't come within a county of any newspaper reporters.

He flipped the newsboy a dime, took his copy, and shook it open. A well-known portrait of him, sketched originally for *Harper's Weekly* and circulated worldwide, gazed off the front page with serene good humor.

Damn, I'm a handsome man, he thought, gazing at himself before he looked at anything else. No wonder Calamity Jane is trying to climb all over me. Poor woman, I'm giving her the night sweats.

Then his eyes flicked to the double-deck head-line:

**WILD BILL RACES NORTH
TO SAVE SIOUX AGAIN!!**

What the hell . . . ? His eyes moved lower, to the byline under the headline: Joshua Robinson.

At this point Hickok was mainly baffled. But by the time he finished the lead paragraph alone, his face was choleric with angry blood.

"Joshua, you little *shit*," he cursed softly, folding the newspaper without reading any more of it. "I'll have your skull for a doorstop, you damned young scamp!"

He had been heading toward Ma Olson's Café for some eats. Now, however, he angled purposely across the street toward the Cattleman's Palace, his thoughts ugly.

Chapter Three

Wild Bill strode across the hotel's fancy lobby, a luxurious clutter of sofas and easy chairs covered in velvet plush with fancy knotted fringe. Even now, mad as he was, Hickok maintained his hairtrigger alertness. His thumbs were curled along the seams of his trousers so he'd be ready to grab iron.

All he drew, however, were several odd stares, for he was still coated with trail grime and required a good bath. Several persons recognized him and sang out, "Touch you for luck, Wild Bill?" Usually he tolerated it with urbane good humor. In his present mood, however, he merely growled back, "Touch a cat's tail."

Bill was so steamed at Josh, he didn't even stop by his own room first to peel off his duster and hat.

"Open up, you little ink-slinging jackass!" he shouted, beating the door of Josh's room with the side of his fist.

The door flew open to reveal a hotel maid, her face a frightened mask.

"*Buenos dias*, Señor Heecock," the Mexican woman stammered.

"Sorry, Maria. Where's the real jackass?"

"Señor Robinson," she replied in Spanglish, "he *es* downstairs *en la cantina. Con un soldado.*"

"With a soldier, huh?" Wild Bill muttered. "Maria, he's gonna need a regiment if he means to avoid me."

Bill headed back downstairs, homicide on his mind. Usually he was one to rile cool. And after all, he had taken a liking to the *New York Herald* reporter, had invited him to tag along and, in effect, widely popularize the legend of Wild Bill Hickok. Hell, the kid even saved his life in Miles City, Montana.

But up to now, Bill thought wryly as he slapped open the batwings that led to the connecting hotel bar, Joshua had only described the cases—now the little pissant was *picking* them.

It was only early afternoon, and the saloon was nearly empty except for a few drummers swapping jokes, their sample cases propped against their legs. Bill spotted Joshua immediately. He was drinking coffee at a table with a young Army lieutenant who, like Josh, looked to be fresh off mother's milk.

Both men were engrossed in their conversation

and failed to notice him enter. Bill headed for the bar first to purchase a bottle of Old Taylor.

Now, however, he confronted a second source of irritation. The latest rage among drinkers was a new cocktail invented by a bartender at the Occidental Hotel in San Francisco—the martini or some damn thing. All Bill cared was that it tied up the bartender all damn day, shaking and mixing the blasted things. Christ sakes, didn't *anybody* drink their liquor neat anymore?

Finally, bottle and jolt glass in hand, he crossed toward the table. Josh saw him coming and instantly paled to the shade of moonstone.

"*There* you are, you clabber-lipped idiot," Bill greeted the reporter. "Kid, some say I'm too quick to put the noose before the gavel. So I mean to be fair—you got anything to say before I shoot you?"

"Wuh—Wild Bill," Josh stammered. "This is Lieutenant Matt Carlson, he—"

"Pleased," Bill said curtly without even looking at the young soldier, who came immediately to attention when he realized: This disheveled, frowning, slightly limping man with the long hair and gunmetal eyes was *the* Wild Bill Hickok— frontier scout under Generals Hancock, Sheridan, and Custer, admired by the most conspicuous soldiers and frontiersmen in America.

"Sir!" the officer popped off like a West Point plebe. "It is a rare pleasure to—"

"Joshua," Bill fumed on, ignoring the soldier and slacking into a chair, "the softest bed I've had in two weeks is pine needles. I've been shot at, stabbed, and punched. My ass is saddle sore and I've swallowed a belly full of trail grit and alkali water. Now I've finally got some gold shiners in my pocket, and I'm looking forward to a little rest and recuperation."

Josh flushed, panic glinting in his eyes. "But you can't!"

Bill flashed him a wicked grin. "Why's that, kid? Might ruin your career, huh? Humiliate your boss back east, Mr. James Gordon Bennett, publishing giant?"

The officer still stood at attention, waiting for the living legend to tell him it was okay to sit.

"Now you tell me," Bill charged on, "just how it comes to pass that I'm organizing a goddamned trail drive to feed a buncha featherheads up north? Naturally I'm just a mite curious, seeing's how I don't know a damn thing about it."

"Well, see, Mr. Pinkerton stopped by to—"

"Pinkerton!"

Bill banged the shot glass to the table and filled it again. "I figured as much, plague take him! That damned promoting fool. He puts Colonel Cody in the shade."

Quickly Josh outlined the dire situation up on the Sioux reservation. He explained how he had no choice—either jump on this important story first, or lose it to competing newspapermen.

Bill stayed silent, letting all this soak in. Slowly he became aware that the young lieutenant still stood at attention, waiting on his command.

"Jesus, Matt, siddown. Cuss, spit, break wind—I ain't an officer anymore."

"Maybe not, sir," Carlson said as he folded his long legs under the table. "But you sure rank high at West Point."

Bill looked at the youth's new gold bars and sighed. The soldier's face was raw from wind and rough soap, beardless, without even one sun crinkle yet. But he had the strong jaw and direct, alert gaze of a man determined to watch and learn. In spite of a foul mood, Bill liked the lad instantly.

"Indian fighter?" Hickok asked.

"Yessir. Well, I haven't actually fought any yet, but I've been trained to do that."

"Indian fighting is pretty much a thing of the past on the Great Plains," Bill assured him. "But if you ever have to engage savages, forget everything they taught you at the Point. It'll just get you killed out here. Especially all that hogwash about 'battle formations.' When you hug with red Arabs, there ain't no front nor rear nor even any flanks. It's running battles—*if* you even see them."

Carlson absorbed every word as if spoken by an oracle. "Forget the Point," he repeated resolutely. "Yessir!"

Now that Bill had noticed Matt, Joshua cleared his throat.

"Matt's on detached assignment from his unit at Fort Trinity," he explained, his eyes running from Hickok's. "He's got a squad of men billeted just east of town—waiting."

"For what?" Hickok upended another jolt of Old Taylor.

The officer looked confused. "Why—waiting on your orders, sir," he explained. He pulled a sheaf of papers out of his tunic and handed them to Hickok.

"The hell's all this?"

"My orders, sir, along with a letter of credit from the U.S. Treasury so you can pay for the cattle, and for supplies, and—"

"Rein it in, Lieutenant," Bill snapped, eyes cutting to Joshua. "You and Pinkerton, huh? You damned fool, don't you see he's just drumming up business for his detectives?"

"Sure, but that's commerce. You said commerce is the soul of the nation."

"It ain't the 'soul of the nation' will be picking lead out of its ass, you knothead. Christ, kid, why'n't you just paint a target on my horse while you're at it? Maybe Pinkerton can pay a couple Chinee kids to hold up a sign that says 'shoot here'!"

For the first time Josh put two facts together: the fact of a $10,000 reward for whoever killed Hickok, and the fact that the newspapers—thanks to telegraphic dispatches—would furnish detailed information on his whereabouts during a cattle drive.

"That's right," Bill said, sharpening the point so the kid would feel it. "Every nickel-chasing, dry-gulching lowlife in the West knows exactly where Hickok can be found."

"Maybe the lowlifes don't read," Josh suggested lamely.

Bill mimicked the kid's voice. "Maybe pigs don't snort, neither."

He took the shot glass between thumb and index finger, tossed back another jolt of bourbon, and finally began to feel himself getting light in the limbs.

"You contact that editor of yours in a puffin' hurry," he told Josh. "Tell him Matt here will be pushing beeves north *without* J. B. Hickok. Tell him this is one time I refuse to boost circulation by serving as the meat that feeds the tiger."

"Bill," Joshua pleaded, "you can't fold up the tent now! Why . . . there's talk around the *Herald* offices about putting my name on the masthead."

"Masthead?" Bill repeated. "How'd we get on a ship all of a sudden?"

"A masthead is the box, inside a newspaper or magazine, where they list the most important names connected with the newspaper. Publisher, editors, and—just sometimes—staff writers."

Bill gave the kid a bleak stare, shaking his head in disgust. "Well, bless my ass! The masthead! Oh, hey, don't *you* fart through silk, Mr. Staff Writer Robinson?"

Josh flushed pink to his earlobes, while Bill poked Matt on the arm.

"How 'bout that, Soldier Blue? Our spelling-bee champ here gets his name on the masthead with all the weak sisters. Well, hell yes, that's worth a fellow getting killed for, ain't it? You'll get *your* name in his newspaper, too, after you're shot full of lead whistlers."

"But, Bill," Josh tried to cut in, "this won't be like that, we—"

"Find somebody with green antlers, kid. Only one thing keeps me from whaling the snot outta you—Pinkerton egged you on. That sly bastard could sell firewood to the devil. But he won't talk me into this cattle drive. I'm taking French leave until I'm broke again."

Wild Bill whacked the cork into his bottle and dropped it into the big front pocket of his duster. He stood up, and Matt rose too. Bill shook the officer's hand.

"Luck to you on this drive, Matt," Hickok told him. "I'll tell you who's a good point rider. Fellow named Jimmy Gruder. Runs a ferry over on the Brazos. An old buffalo soldier, used to scout for the Cavalry before the war."

By now, realizing Bill meant it, Josh had turned pale as fresh linen. This was going to make the country's greatest newspaper look foolish—reduce it to the same scandalous level of the gossipy "penny papers" sold all over New York City.

"Bill," he protested, "you can't—"

"Lads, enjoyed our little palaver," Hickok called over his shoulder as he walked off. "Now, if you'll excuse me—I need to soak loose a few layers of Texas topsoil."

For ten cents the hotel bathhouse furnished a big tub of hot water, soap, and a clean towel. For a nickel extra, an excellent barber across the street shaved you afterward, including a splash of bay rum tonic.

Wild Bill picked his favorite tub, one with a clear view of the entire room and the only door. A rusty iron stove on brick legs, lit only in winter, covered his back.

He had already stopped by his room for a clean change of clothing. Now he stripped and tossed his dirty laundry into a canvas hamper for the housekeeping staff. He left his shell belt dangling from a gilded hook on the wall, both ivory butts ready to hand.

Before he eased into the steaming water, Bill skinned off the paper wrapper of a cheroot. He lit a phosphor with his thumbnail, got the cigar going good, then set his bottle of Old Taylor where he could reach it without effort.

"Sweet Jasmine Brown," he said in a soft sigh, relaxing in the warm bath. Numerous old injuries—bullet and knife wounds, broken bones, bear maulings, and the like—made a hot soak even more gratifying.

The door banged open, and Bill had a fist around a .44 before the echo ceased. It was only the young *mestizo* kid who was in charge of emptying the hamper. Bill dropped the gun back into its hand-tooled holster before the lad even knew it had been aimed at him.

"Cattle drive," Hickok said out loud, though the kid was gone and he was alone in the big bathhouse. "Trying to make a damned cow nurse outta me."

Bill conceded that cowboys were a skilled bunch rendering a great service to the nation. But it was an ascetic, stoic life, and a hell of a way to make low wages—half the pay of a sheepherder. All his life he had justified the various hardships he encountered by telling himself at least it was better than whipping beeves on the butt like some common waddie.

This time, when the door opened, it was smooth and quiet.

Again Wild Bill drew steel, thumbing the hammer back.

"Please don't shoot me in the face," the intruder pleaded. "I hope to leave a beautiful corpse."

An ear-to-ear grin stretched Bill's face wide. He holstered his Colt, watching the new arrival where she stood just inside the door. A sign outside clearly said "Men," but he could ignore it if she could, hell yes.

"C'mon in, Ida," he invited her. "Water's warm."

Ida Gipson made a little moue. "It might get a little *too* warm," she hinted, "with two of us in that bitty tub."

"Oh, I guarantee it will."

Bill leveled appreciative eyes on the singer. She was a fiery-haired, emerald-eyed beauty with a girl's face, but a woman's knowledge when she looked at a man the way she looked at Bill now.

Ida sang across the street at the Lone Star Saloon, where she was well-liked and well-paid. Bill admired the way tight stays and a lace corset shoved her breasts up on tempting display—breasts as ivory white and smooth as the butts of his .44s.

"I was returning to my room when I saw you come in here," she explained. "I wanted to be sure to catch you before you rode out on this new mission to feed the starving Indians up north. It's a *noble* thing you're doing, Bill."

Her manner made it very clear that "noble" men melted her resistance.

"Ahhm—why, thanks," Bill replied, catching himself just in time before he told her he wasn't going.

"I confess, Bill, I've been slow to respond to your . . . attentions because of the things people say."

"Such as . . . ?"

"Oh, how you're a cold-blooded killer," she flung at him bluntly.

"Should I be *passionate* about ending a life?"

Her pretty face went blank with surprise. But she joined him in a good laugh—his joke came wrapped in a truism.

"Anyway," he added, "I save my warmer blood for more pleasant occasions."

Bill abruptly decided he would seem more gallant if he took the cigar from his teeth.

"What's that?" he added, pointing with his chin at the book tucked under her arm.

"Oh, just light reading for self-improvement. It's Colonel Thompson's fascinating book about wild horses."

Those emerald eyes held him as she added: "Did you know, Wild Bill, that only the fittest stallions get to breed? I didn't realize the mares were so choosy."

"They are," Hickok agreed, "but quite, ahh, eager once they've chosen."

She flushed, but held the gaze. "That makes sense to me—once she's chosen, I mean."

Despite the opportunity that was obviously knocking, Bill couldn't shake the damned irony of it. Joshua's presumptuous story had thawed Ida quicker than liquor. Was this typical of the way American women were interpreting this feed-the-Sioux angle?

"Ooops! Somebody's coming," she said, adding quickly before she left: "I was hoping we might . . . visit a bit before you leave. I'm one floor below you in number seventeen."

She slipped out, and a moment later the *mestizo* kid was back, this time to stock the supplies of soap and towels. Bill's grin lingered until he realized something: Word would get out quick once he turned down this consarned cattle drive job. Maybe even so quick that Ida might . . .

Something else occurred to him. Something even more important than a dalliance with Ida. So far it was his highly publicized fearlessness that stayed the hands of ninety-nine out of a hundred men who might like to kill the famous Hickok.

So now, wasn't he trapped? Josh had committed him. If Hickok said no, it would look to the God-almighty public like he was "backing out," not just refusing. And that would send the worst possible message—that he had snow in his boots.

Truth to tell, he did. But Bill knew he dare not admit it. Once the newspapers turned on him, even *hinting* there was a chink in his armor, fortune hunters would descend on him like a plague of locusts. Hell, the cross fire alone would kill him.

"Damnitall, anyway," Bill said out loud. "Now it's out, I *have* to do it."

"Mozo," he called over to the kid. "When you leave, send a messenger in here, *sabes*? Send two."

"*Sí*, Señor Hee-cock."

Bill decided he'd best send word out to those soldiers, tell them not to pull their picket pins just yet. He also wanted to put a possible cattle seller on notice.

"Damn you, Joshua, you win," Bill muttered as he began furiously sudsing under one arm. "But just you wait until you find out what it'll cost you, sonny boy."

Chapter Four

It was true that Wild Bill could be a notorious wastrel. But once he went broke, sobered up, and took the bit in his teeth again, he pulled straight for the homestretch.

"Let's get this show on the road, drovers!" he shouted early the next morning as he burst into Joshua's room at 5 A.M. sharp.

The reporter shouted back in protest when the unwelcome intruder threw back the warm covers.

"Drop it and grab your socks, Sleeping Beauty, we got to buy one thousand head of cattle today and put 'em on some grass by sundown."

"You mean—"

"I mean today the Philadelphia Kid becomes a cowboy."

Josh, several cowlicks giving him a rooster's

crown, came fully awake and sat up. "Man alive! You're gonna *do* it, Bill?"

"Your name'll go in that damned masthead," Hickok assured him. "But since I'm playing your tune, *you* will damn well pay the piper. You're going along."

"*Course* I'm going along—I'm telling the story. And since I'm actually *on* the drive, I get the story before any other newspaperman. Jeepers!"

"Oh, you'll be on the drive, all right. Matter fact, you're gonna have one job the whole way."

Josh paled, for he was an excellent "trail chef," as Bill called him. That's one of the reasons he's tolerated me this long, Josh thought.

"Not the cook?" he whined.

Bill shook his head as the kid hurriedly dressed in his only set of range clothes, all brand-spanking new.

"Worse," Hickok promised. "The cook is a high-ranking man on a trail drive and takes few orders. You'll be riding the drag slot, junior. It'll be your job to serve as guard along our backtrail while also prodding the laggard cows along."

Josh gave a no-big-deal shrug. "Doesn't sound so bad. I've worked on a Kansas railroad gang and a Black Hills mining crew since I've been side-kicking with you. This can't be worse."

Bill held his face in a deadpan only with effort. "Gets a mite dusty back there," he said mildly.

"Dust? Huh, big deal."

Obviously, Bill told himself, this mere chit of a

51

lad had no idea how much dust cattle raised on a dry Texas trail in July. He'd soon find out what a "big deal" it was.

"Some of the cattle will be lured into the brush by *ladinos*," Bill added. "You'll have to haze them out."

The kid stabbed his shirttail into his copper-riveted Levi's, still stiff as cardboard. "What's a *ladino*?"

"Wild cow," Bill said. "They like to hide in the brushy country, bushwhack humans."

Josh laughed. "Wild cows? This is a joke like with snipe, right? I suppose these wild cows eat humans too, huh?"

"Nope. They just like to trample and gore them," Bill replied.

Josh ignored this silly joke, eager to be filled in.

"Why'd you change your mind?" he demanded. "Pinkerton?"

Bill snorted. "Pinkerton is conveniently out of town—evidently, about the same time I rode into San Antone, he lit a shuck for Brownsville. 'On business.'"

"If it wasn't Pinkerton, then—"

Josh paused, recalling something. He had stopped by Bill's room several times last night, but no one answered, not even at midnight, when Josh finally turned in.

"Say! Ida didn't show up for her act last night," Josh said, thinking out loud. "And you were no-where to be found. Everybody knows Ida is a big champion of Indian rights."

"I found that out myself," Bill admitted. "Kid, you've got a mind like a steel trap. But you've got a round ass in the saddle. Those boots are brand new and useless for cowpunching. They've got no heels—how will you hold the stirrups when your horse is cutting sharp? We'll buy you some at the mercantile when I lay in some new rope."

"How 'bout my hat?" Josh showed him a new straw Sonora.

"It'll do, but watch it in the wind. I'd tie on a chin string. First chance you get, sew a rag on the back, too, to cover your neck. That Texas sun'll fry you to leather."

All business establishments, except the bank, opened at sunrise, which was still a half hour off. The two men first stopped by the livery to rig Bill's roan and Josh's coyote dun. Bill checked the shoes on both animals and inspected their hooves for any cracks or embedded stones.

"These two are fine," Bill remarked, turning to cinch his latigos. "But we'll still need a remuda for the trail. The workday is long, and each man should have at least three horses so he can spell off. Did Matt bring any?"

"Yeah, but he calls it the cavvy, not the remuda. Twenty extra horses."

"Won't be enough," Bill complained. "And they'll be them overfed, underworked Army nags."

The two friends led their saddled mounts outside into the gray light of dawn.

"They're trained not to panic under fire," Bill

added, still thinking about the Army remounts, "but they'll be useless for hazing cows."

By now Ma Olsen's Café was open. The two men enjoyed a hearty meal of eggs, potatoes, ham, and biscuits. Then they stopped by the mercantile, where Josh bought new boots, work gloves, eye-shades, petroleum jelly, and other items Bill told him were useful on a cattle trail.

"We'll stop by and pick up our cowboys in blue," Bill said sarcastically as they left the store. "Then we'll go buy the beef."

"You got a seller in mind?"

Bill nodded. "I'm a doer, not a dreamer. Fellow south of town—I've done some work for his brother's freighting company. Saw one of his cowboys in town last night, so I sent a message out to him."

Hickok swung up into leather and kicked his right foot into the stirrup. "Fellow named Dolph Reynolds, owns the Four Sixes brand south of here. Beef supplier during the Great Rebellion, too, so he's used to government contracts. Brags how he always has at least a few thousand head on hand for quick sale."

Matt Carlson and his detail were camped in a pine-sheltered hollow two miles west of town. By the time Bill and Josh arrived, the soldiers had broken camp and were standing by as per Bill's orders sent the day before.

Wild Bill cast a jaundiced eye over the small formation of men as they stood at parade rest for his initial inspection. As soldiers, they looked fairly squared away—reasonably clean uniforms and good morale.

As cowboys, however, they did not inspire much hope at first glance. Bill quickly checked their hands: no rope calluses on any of them. Nor had they been allowed to bring their new Spencer carbines along, an excellent defensive weapon. Instead they had been issued old parade-deck weapons, ranging from brass-framed Henry rifles to early-model Volcanic and Winchester lever-action repeaters. Bill doubted if all of them worked.

"Any of you men know how to tie a double-hitch knot?" Bill asked them.

Silence.

"Any of you know how to use a piggin' string?"

More silence until someone said, "We're herding pigs?"

"Jesus Katy Christ Almighty," Bill swore, but with a calm precision that made it sound solemn. "Can one of you gentlemen, just one, rope and drop a Longhorn?"

The silence became almost deafening. Wild Bill stared at Matt. "Lieutenant, I thought these men knew cattle."

Matt flushed. "There was a little mix-up at the fort, sir. The company clerk mistakenly sent that group out on a road-building detail. These road builders were all I had left to take."

"I've milked cows, Wild Bill," volunteered a tall, gangly corporal wearing an eye patch. "My name's Abel Langford, grew up on a farm in Iowa."

"Least you'll know a cow from a bull," Bill conceded. "That's a start."

"I know cows good enough to butcher 'em," spoke up a private beside Abel. "I used to butcher and cook for a railroad gang."

Bill snapped his fingers and grinned. "Now we're whistling! What's your name, son?"

"Private Rob Meadows, sir."

"You're going to sling the hash. Matt?"

"Yessir!"

Bill pointed to the buckboard wagon being used to haul hay and other supplies.

"I'm commandeering that vehicle for our chuck wagon. Private Meadows is going to stay behind today with one man to help him. Somebody who's strong and good with tools. That buckboard has to be reinforced for the trail."

"Swede!" Matt sang out. "You'll be cook's assistant."

Quickly Bill instructed Meadows and Swede, a big, strapping lad with thighs like thick trees, where to nail a big wooden box onto the back of the buckboard to hold food supplies and medicine for the trail. And how to reinforce the axles with rope bracings.

"Rig a cowhide sling underneath the wagon, too," he added. "Use it to store sticks and cow chips. Otherwise, you'll have no kindling out on the open flats. This route is scarce on wood."

Wild Bill had one remaining item of business before riding south to buy cattle: explaining the route they would all be following for the long, hard weeks ahead. Bill knew, from personal experience in the Army, that soldiers performed better when they knew exactly where they were going, and when.

"Men, we'll be taking Chisholm's Trail most of the way north. It was first opened by Jesse Chisholm in '67. Lots of folks confuse him with New Mexico cattleman John Chisum—no relation. The trail originates deep in the Live Oak country, between the Rio Grande and the Nueces Rivers."

Bill pointed over his shoulder. "We'll pick up the trail just east of San Antone. We'll bear more or less due north through the Indian Territory to Caldwell on the Kansas border. The trail forks there. The right branch aims for the railhead at Abilene, the left terminates in Ellsworth."

Josh felt a shudder move down his spine at mention of Abilene. Last time they were there, he and Bill had barely made it out of that hellhole alive. So he welcomed Hickok's next words.

"But we'll pass up both railheads. We've got to keep shoving north until we hit Nelson Story's old trail in southern Nebraska. That'll take us northwest to the reservation just past Ogallala. Any questions?"

"What'll the terrain be like?" asked Corporal Langford. "Have you covered it before?"

Bill nodded. "Plenty of times. We'll be spared the worst badlands found farther west—those dead and barren expanses so dry you'll find only lizards and insects. Still, there'll be some long dry stretches. Like the ride between the Colorado and the Brazos Rivers."

Otis Jones, a Negro sergeant wearing several battle decorations, asked: "Any hostiles along this route, Wild Bill?"

Bill sent a withering stare at Joshua, who flushed and began examining his new boots.

"The Indians are all mostly pacified by now, Sarge," Hickok replied. "But I'm told somebody up north has good reasons for stopping the Sioux from getting this beef. And there's a good chance somebody will be trying to plug me, too, but that's my lookout, not yours. You men just watch after those cows, keep them moving, and keep them alive."

That'll be hard enough, Josh was beginning to fully realize. Not one of these soldiers was a "cowboy" or anything close to one. Several, in fact, were merely young, green recruits from back east. Thank God they were at least Cavalry troops, and could thus handle a horse—or so he hoped.

"All right!" Bill called out. "We're burning daylight, Matt. Since you're the officer in charge, you'll also serve as my ramrod for the drive. Get your men mounted, and we'll go meet our cows."

Dolph Reynolds's spread was located an hour's ride south of San Antonio. His big ranch was typical of those in South Texas: some forty thousand cattle roaming a million acres of open range, much of it cactus and mesquite brush.

Old Dolph's fires were banked by now, but the

venerable cattleman could still sit a saddle straight and proud. He rode out with his visitors, accompanied by his *caporal*, or foreman, to supervise the sale.

The *caporal* ordered some of the hands to cut a thousand head off the main gather and group them in a dusty wash nearby for more precise counting by the soldiers.

"You men!" Matt called out to his troopers. "Keep a sharp eye out and watch how these cowboys handle the Longhorns. We'll all have to learn quick, sort of on the hoof."

Hearing this, Dolph stared at Hickok. The old bird savored snuff in his upper lip, slurring his speech slightly.

"Bill, did I hear that shavetail right? These men have never punched cattle?"

Bill pointed at Josh with his chin. "This little miss right here is my drag rider, Dolph. Does that answer your question?"

Josh felt heat flood into his face. The old Texan squinted dubiously as he took in the skinny young city whippersnapper. Joshua had met Dolph's type many times in cattle country. He was not a bad man, but hard and unbending.

"Looks like a damn soft-mouthed schoolteacher," Dolph growled. "White as a fish belly. He'll never make it. None of 'em will, Bill. They'll never reach Red River Station. Them as don't drown in the Colorado will drown in the Brazos or the Trinity."

Josh felt anger stir in his belly, but he said nothing. He followed Matt's advice and paid close attention to the seasoned cowboys as they bunched the cattle in the wash, making it look easy.

"You'll need *pochos* for this job," Dolph assured Hickok.

Pochos was the name Mexicans from the interior used for gringos who worked cattle this deep in Texas. The *pochos* all rode excellent cow ponies, much smaller than the Cavalry mounts. Agile cutters, able to dodge quicker than the longhorns.

Constantly slapping their chaps and making shrill yipping noises, Dolph's veteran punchers made bossing cows around seem like a trip to Santa's lap. The longhorns, healthy but not fat, were typical of the hardy breed: brindle or muddy black, some with horns spreading up to seven feet. All had four 6's burned across their ribs.

Josh noticed, as few others did, how vigilant Hickok had become around the *pochos*. He had discreetly knocked the riding thongs off his .44s. And he had his eye on one man in particular, an excellent roper who was subduing some bulls that refused to be hazed.

The man had inscrutable Indian features, but sandy hair and piercing blue eyes. What got Bill's attention, however, were the Navy Colts tied low.

"No cowboy ties down his short gun," Bill remarked quietly to Josh. "That's an invitation to be braced."

"He sure looks like a cowboy," Josh admired, watching the man work resin into his gloves before expertly settling a loop of rope over a long spread of horns.

"What you're looking at right now," Bill explained, "is the Mexican floating-rope style called dally roping. Notice how most of the others just flip the rope hard and fast without floating it? That's Texas style."

"Judging from the soldiers' faces," Josh said, "they don't know either style."

"Longfellow, them soldiers don't know a cow's ass from its horns. If we get across the first river, I'll eat my hat. Even their saddles are all wrong for working cattle. See how the cowboy saddles have that narrow, twelve-inch cantle? That lets you—"

Wild Bill never finished his sentence. Even his hair-trigger reflexes were too slow when the dally roper, who had been on the verge of roping another longhorn, suddenly dropped his spinning lariat over Hickok instead!

The rest was a matter of mere moments. The rope tightened hard, pinning Bill's arms below the elbows and close to his sides. Before Josh could even credit his own eyes, Wild Bill was tugged violently off his roan.

His captor dug his rowels into the back of an Indian cayuse. With all the dust, noise, and activity, few others even noticed, at first, when Hickok started bouncing and flying around like a bundle of rags as the cowboy's horse raced toward a patch of prickly pear.

Cold revulsion filled Josh's belly when he realized something: His glory-seeking headline had put the first reward hunter after Wild Bill.

Matt, too, spotted the trouble when it was too late. The soldier had his rifle out of the scabbard in two shakes. But Josh saw it was hopeless—the savvy rider was holding a zigzag pattern as he receded, providing a poor target.

Luckily, Wild Bill never counted on anyone to save his bacon. Somehow, just before he would have been savagely torn apart in the cactus, he managed to get one gun out and shoot through the rope.

He rolled over and over until he stopped, bloody and bruised, only yards from the cactus patch. But he was still in great danger. Tied as he was, he could "aim" only by awkwardly shifting his entire body, and then it was the crudest aim.

The *pocho* wheeled his horse, jerked the Remington repeater from his saddle boot, and threw the butt into his shoulder hollow, levering a shell into the chamber.

Matt shot at him and missed. The *pocho*, fierce and quick like a badger, opened fire on Bill as he charged, a hail of lead kicking up dust geysers all around him. Somehow Bill managed to plug the charging horse, and with a violent shudder in midair, it collapsed.

But this *pocho* was battle savvy. He lifted his legs clear so he wouldn't be pinned by the dying horse. He continued on foot, levering and firing, relentless in his attack. Obviously he knew the caliber of man he faced, and had no plans to give Hickok the slightest chance.

All Bill's attacker needed to do, to get out of the line of fire, was veer sharply every time Bill got set. But even thus stymied, Josh marveled, Hickok refused to quit fighting. He was "ear aiming" now, trying to kill the cowboy by the sound of his rifle, the scuff of his boots.

Matt tried to fire again, but his carbine—probably dust-clogged in all this haze—jammed on him. He was desperately trying to clear the stoppage when a pistol roared behind them, and the *pocho* froze in his tracks, looking up at the sky in shocked surprise.

Blood spurted from a neat hole in the middle of his forehead, his knees abruptly came unhinged, and he crumpled dead into the dust, heels scratching the dirt a few times.

All heads, including Wild Bill's, craned around to stare at a sight so ludicrous they all instantly forgot the gun battle: A homely, stout woman wearing a red bandanna and leather chaps sat astride a camel almost as ugly as she was. An immaculate gray Stetson was the only clean item of clothing the prairie hag wore. A Smith & Wesson she poked back into her red sash was still smoking.

"Wal, cut off my legs and call me Shorty!" Martha "Calamity Jane" Burke roared out in a voice like the mating call of a bull moose. "Bill Hickok, my soul alive! What are you doing flat on your ass with sons of bitches trying to plug you?"

Chapter Five

"Confound it, woman, if that's what you are," growled Dolph, fighting to control his frightened horse. "Get that ugly hunchback donkey the hell back—it's spooking the horses!"

"No need go get your nose out of joint, Methuselah," Jane assured him. "Ignatius is well-behaved, just like me."

To prove it, the camel suddenly spat with expert aim, tagging the disgusted old cattle baron smack in the left cheek.

"Serves you right for calling him a donkey," Jane told Dolph brashly, watching Joshua loosen the rope that pinned Wild Bill's arms. The cowboys and soldiers had all ceased working to gawk at the new arrivals. Everyone kept his nervous horse well back.

Josh had done a feature story last year on the

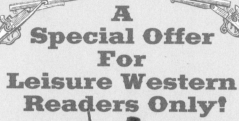

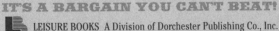

GET YOUR 4 FREE* BOOKS NOW— A VALUE BETWEEN $16 AND $20

Mail the Free* Book Certificate Today!

FREE* BOOKS CERTIFICATE!

YES! I want to subscribe to the Leisure Western Book Club. Please send me my 4 FREE* BOOKS. Then, each month, I'll receive the four newest Leisure Western Selections to preview FREE* for 10 days. If I decide to keep them, I will pay the Special Member's Only discounted price of just $3.36 each, a total of $13.44 ($14.50 US in Canada). This saves me between $3 and $6 off the bookstore price. There are no shipping, handling or other charges.* There is no minimum number of books I must buy and I may cancel the program at any time. In any case, the 4 FREE* BOOKS are mine to keep—at a value of between $17 and $20!

*In Canada, add $5.00 Canadian shipping and handling per order for first shipment. For all subsequent shipments to Canada the cost of membership in the Book Club is $14.50 US, which includes $7.50 shipping and handling per month. All payments must be made in US currency.

Name _____

Address _____

City_____ State_____ Country_____

Zip_____ Telephone_____

Tear here and mail your FREE* book card today!

Get Four Books Totally
F R E E* —
A Value between
$16 and $20

Tear here and mail your FREE* book card today!

PLEASE RUSH
MY FOUR FREE*
BOOKS TO ME
RIGHT AWAY!

LeisureWestern Book Club
P.O. Box 6613
Edison, NJ 08818-6613

AFFIX
STAMP
HERE

Army's now mostly disbanded Camel Corps. The hearty animals proved too ill-tempered and spiteful for most of the Army's needs. Besides which, they terrified hell out of every horse that saw them. But a small herd was still maintained as pack animals for special desert operations such as resupplying remote mirror stations in the Mojave and Sonora country.

"I see you're still working for the Army," Bill told Jane as he quickly checked to make sure the dead roper was not a possum player. His next act, also a habit by now, was to thumb reloads into the spent chambers of his .44s.

"I'm Uncle Sam's official Camel Keeper," Jane boasted, nudging her hat back. "We got our own ranch in the Pecos River Valley in New Mexico Territory. But I put my Indian helper in charge and hightailed it here the minute I heard you're pushing up the Chisholm Trail—and parading the fact all over hell," she added in a disapproving tone. "See what all that newspaper claptrap does for you, Bill?"

Joshua felt guilty, for already somebody had tried to cash in on Bill's hide, and it was partly the reporter's fault. But he had to bite his lip to keep a straight face.

Wild Bill had just faced a blazing gun without breaking a sweat. Now, however, Calamity Jane's lovestruck gaze made sweat pour down his face.

"I don't want that nickel-chasing scalper buried in my dirt," Dolph told his *caporal*, staring at the corpse on the ground. "My wife lies in that ground, and she was one of the few Christians in Texas. Just toss him out on the open range and let the buzzards bury him."

Dolph growled at the rest of his gawping men: "This ain't no hurdy-gurdy show—get them beeves bunched!"

Dolph's hands went back to hazing cattle while Matt's beleaguered soldiers did their best to count and hold them.

Josh gave Bill a hand up. Ignoring various scrapes and cuts, the dandified frontiersman grumped about the holes worn into his new whip-cord trousers.

"Bill Hickok," Jane said in a stern, lecturing tone, "what in tarnal blazes were you thinking when you announced, in every damned newspaper in America, right where you'll be for the next month or so?"

"Ask Mr. Golden Quill," Bill replied, nodding toward Josh. "Jane, meet the Masthead Kid. He's using my gravestone as a rung on the ladder of success."

"That little chit ain't all to blame," Jane snapped at her beloved. "I never seen Bill Hickok grow modest around an ink-slinger. Anyhow, soon's I heard, I knew I'd have to tag along and shoot some jaspers."

"Tag along," Bill repeated woodenly, his hands suddenly itching to take Joshua by the gullet.

"Why, shore! I tole you before, good-lookin', that we got us a *shared* destiny. Haven't I yanked your hams from the fire before?"

The plug-ugly Jane flashed him a smile full of gaps and tobacco-stained, broken teeth.

Dolph was old and cantankerous, but a sharp weather vane for humor. Josh saw him openly smirking at the entertaining turn this trail was taking.

Taking a cue from his boss, one of the cowboys called out slyly: "Bunkhouse is empty, you two lovebirds."

Bill had the look of a condemned man, and Josh knew why. It didn't matter how coyote ugly Jane was, or that she smelled like a buffalo wallow on a humid day. The truth was she *had* saved Bill's bacon, and more than once. Bill had once summed up the irony of it when he called her "my guardian angel from hell."

As much as the perfumed dandy and Lothario of the frontier hated to admit it—his destiny did indeed seem linked to Calamity Jane by some higher power. But damnitall, Hickok thought, the woman scares the Jesus out of me.

"Well," Bill finally replied to her, his tone resigned, "you'll have to hang back a piece, Jane. We can't have Ignatius spooking the cattle and horses. Most especial, not when I'll have so many greenhorns working cattle."

At these words, Wild Bill sent a sly, slanted glance at Joshua. "Kid, you'll be riding drag—closest to Jane," he clarified in a goading tone. "Maybe she can help you with . . . well, you know."

Jane, who had long considered Josh "a cute little parcel of manflesh," demanded: "Help Joshua with what?"

"Oh, you know how it is, Jane," Bill said in a confidential voice. "The lad's in his prime, fit as a stag in season. But he's still . . . uninitiated, if you take my drift?"

Jane, far less delicate than Bill, turned lascivious eyes on the quaking newspaperman.

"Joshua, do you mean to tell me you *still* ain't had your package wrapped?"

"I . . . uh, that is, you see—"

"What Little Boy Blush is trying to say," Bill took over, "is that he's a little nervous about his first ride—you know, about staying in the saddle long enough?"

"Why, hell 'n' furies! Eight seconds can win the rodeo," Jane assured the beet-red youth. "It's easy as finding your own pee hole! C'mon, I'll take you out in the bushes right now and get you broke in proper."

"Shoot, I gotta go help with the cattle," Josh blurted, quickly wheeling his dun and joining the dusty pandemonium.

Bill's grin faded when he realized Jane had fixed her mating eye on him again.

"If you two need to be alone," Dolph offered from a crusty deadpan, "I can—"

"Time's pushing," Bill cut him off in a hurry. "I'll take that bill of sale, Dolph, and we'll be on our way."

* * *

About 850 miles to the north, Jip and Olney Lucas were making life miserable for the reservation Sioux in Nebraska. They had become adept at their work.

"Hell, pour all of it in there," Olney encouraged his older brother. "We can get plenty more from Harding."

Jip, his chinless, completely common face focused on his task, stood among a stand of cattails, ankle deep in water. He shook white powder from a big bucket into a shallow pool of clear water. There was plenty of subsurface moisture, on this choice section of the rez, and it was a simple matter to regularly poison the game-watering holes with powerful strychnine.

"Them red niggers can set all the snares they want," Olney added. "Any game they find around here will be too dead to skin."

"Wunst the Injuns're gone," Jip tossed in, as if rehearsing the steps to himself, "we stop the poisoning."

"Yeah-boy! Game'll be back in no time."

Deerflies pestered both men and their horses. But insects were among the last signs of abundant life in this area—insects and a few ground-nesting birds such as scaled quail and prairie chickens.

A few short months ago, this part of southwestern Nebraska had teemed with wildlife: badgers, beavers, foxes, muskrats, raccoons, bigger game like antelopes, plenty of red-tailed hawks, and meadowlarks. Now it was as empty and desolate as Nevada's Black Rock Desert, where the Lucas boys had been born and abandoned. They were raised by a missionary family they eventually robbed and murdered.

"Hey, Olney?"

"Hay is for horses."

Jip, still shaking poison into the water, said: "You figure Harding was on the level about Woman Dress?"

"What? You mean about lettin' us two have a whack at her now and then?"

"Un-hunh. Only, he said anytime we wanted to, not now and then."

"Big brother, no man means everything he says. We can't just up and top her any old time we get the itch. Hell, I'd be over there every damn day liftin' up her skirt! But is he talking the straight about lettin' us have some sweet stuff now and then? Hell yes!"

"Sure," Jip said, reasoning it out. "Why not? It ain't like she's his wife or a white woman. He paid for her, didn't he? He might as well get some use outta her. We can have her when he's too busy."

"Anh-hanh," Olney replied absently, for Jip was a half-wit and didn't care what he said anyway. Olney bothered to keep an eye out now and then, just in case Federal troops paid a surprise visit.

The country surrounding the Lucas boys was endless and more of the same in every direction: open, green, and so vast it shimmered on the horizon. So vast, too, that there was no clear demarcation between near and far, no clear sense where the foreground transformed into background. The only reference points were a few small cabins of cottonwood logs chinked with mud. They had recently replaced the traditional buffalo-hide tepees. The Sioux had no choice once Uncle Pte, the buffalo, was virtually wiped out.

"That'll do 'er at this end," Olney announced as his brother emptied the bucket and waded ashore. "Now we can get set to ride south and put the quietus on this cattle drive."

Their destructive labors, up here, went far beyond merely poisoning water holes. First they made sure to intimidate the freighters who delivered the tribe's government rations. They had also torn up any traplines they discovered. Likewise, they destroyed all the brush dams Sioux farmers had thrown up across feeder creeks and streams to irrigate gardens.

By now, with the exception of Chinook, Bobcat, and the well-fed reservation police force, the Sioux were facing starvation. The children, especially, were in trouble because the few cows still alive were sick and gave thin milk with blood in it.

"Harding is happy as a fly on a turd," Olney said while the two men removed the hobbles from their mounts. "The Sioux Headmen are meeting in council today to vote on whether they should move south of the Platte. Their medicine men are saying this part is cursed land because of a big buffalo slaughter two years back."

The two brothers hit leather, whirled their mounts, and headed back toward their dirt soddy located just off federal land. Before Harding Ott hired them as his "field assistants," the brothers ran an illegal still right on the edge of the reservation. They had brewed whiskey from gunpowder and tobacco and sold it by the cup to any Indians who had something worth trading.

"Riders coming this way," Olney remarked, for his eyes missed little. He loosened both of his Colt Lightnings in their holsters. But a few minutes later, he announced: "It's Bobcat and Chinook. They're heading for the council lodge at Crying Woman Creek."

Although technically the two white men were trespassing, they had nothing to fear. Chinook, Harding Ott's lapdog, was merely a show chief. He had been put in power by Ott, who had killed Chief Catch the Bear for the crime of being incorruptible. By the time of the killing, the rest of the tribe was too weakened by hunger to organize any resistance.

"How you two warriors doing today?" Olney greeted the Sioux, his tone mocking the word "warriors."

Both braves reined in. Only they and the policemen had horses—the rest had eaten their ponies by now. These two also wore white man's clothing except for their moccasins. But their long black hair reeked of bear fat. In recognition of the Council's importance, it was braided with strips of colored cloth.

Chinook, with his gaunt face seamed by many hard winters, seemed like a strong, resolute brave at first glance—a mature but still vigorous leader. However, behind that imposing exterior dwelled a weak, easily led man.

"Hey, Chinook," Olney greeted the older Sioux. "You fellows out seeking a vision from Great Ussen?"

"Great Ussen," said Bobcat, whose English was better than Chinook's, "is Apache god, not Lakota."

"Well now, pardon me all to hell and back."

Bobcat, like all the reservation policemen under him, carried a good-condition Hotchkiss bolt-action carbine in his saddle boot, supplied by Ott and forbidden by treaty. It was a trim, deadly-looking weapon with no frills.

Bobcat exchanged a secretive glance with Chinook.

"You have not heard," he said to Olney, "about the whites coming by the Cattle Road with meat for the Lakota people?"

"Course we've heard, blanket ass," Jip replied. "We was right there when Ott told you about it."

Again the two braves traded glances, their impassive faces revealing nothing. But the Lucas boys weren't worried—they were backed by Olney's puma reflexes and Sam Colt's genius. And even before Olney cleared a holster, his dullard-looking brother could get the ten-inch "frog-sticker" out of his boot—and toss it through a man's heart at thirty paces.

However, such deadly skills were not needed. Chinook and Bobcat, while differing sharply in temperament, had both concluded that the red man's glory was over.

Resistance was deadly folly. These hair-faces from places beyond the seas—their numbers made them like ants from giant colonies, too numerous to kill. Only look at Sitting Bull, Chief Joseph, or any Indian fool enough to fight the pale ones. Even the High Holy Ones of Indian belief had sided with the white men. Any tribe who fought them—look how their medicine had gone bad. Even mighty Geronimo, now running like a scared rabbit.

"No," Bobcat finally said. "You do not take my meaning. We have just seen Harding Ott at the trading post. The white man's talking sheets"—he meant newspapers—"are filled by the news."

"What news, you damned old gossip?" Olney demanded impatiently. Indians were the god*damn*dest people to get anything out of.

"The white man called Ice Shaman by the Lakota," Bobcat replied, "will lead the yellow-legs on the Cattle Road."

"So what? Who in bleeding Christ is the Ice Shaman?"

"Your people know him," Bobcat said, "as Wild Bill Hickok."

At this intelligence, both Lucas boys stared at each other.

"Horseshit," Jip challenged.

Bobcat shrugged an indifferent shoulder. "So? Then Ott speaks bent words like all white men.

This is what he said. And what he told me to tell you."

Olney had remained silent. Now he said, "It's prob'ly the truth, Jip. See, Hickok is a whatcha-callit, a Pinkerton man now. And Mr. Pinkerton's got him an office down in the Texas cattle country."

Olney looked at Bobcat, trying to read his face. "How's Harding taking the news?"

Again Bobcat lifted one shoulder. "His will is an iron fist. He showed no concern."

"What, you sayin' I am?"

Olney's left hand held his bunched reins. But the right cupped a holster, ready to murder any man—red, white, or polka dot—who insulted him.

Bobcat shook his head. "You are not afraid, no. But the Ice Shaman will kill you. His medicine is strong."

The two braves nudged their ponies and moved on.

"His 'medicine' ain't worth a cup of cold piss!" Olney shouted behind them. "And the only thing 'strong' is the smell of all that manure you two shovel!"

Chapter Six

Dolph Reynolds's hands had bunched the cows, then quickly cut them out by parcels for the official count. Now the deal was sealed. It was up to "Wild Bill's Blue-Bloused Waddies"—as one newspaper wag had already dubbed the soldiers—to push them north out of Texas.

Josh could tell from Hickok's bemused face that he still didn't quite believe *he* was in charge of this dog-and-pony show. True enough, Wild Bill had long observed cowboys at their craft, even in the days before they became familiar cultural heroes. But he had never actually done any cow hazing himself. And if at all possible, he meant to continue not doing it.

Insofar as he could, he meant to supervise only. Like most of these confused soldiers, he possessed no roping skills. But he was in charge and had to hide his ignorance. Besides, Wild Bill knew that, mainly, a cowboy simply needed endurance—the endurance of a doorknob. The rest could be learned.

Although, he admitted, a little luck would be nice too. Especially at the many river crossings. More cowboys died drowning in these rivers than from all other causes. The same would no doubt hold true for soldiers, too, so long as they were doing a cowboy's job. An amazing number of frontier men never learned to swim.

"Start riding a slow, easy circle around the herd to hold them," Bill instructed Abel Langford, the tall corporal with the eye patch. "Keep them bunched tight. But hold your mount to a walk, and don't shout or make any sudden noise. And *do not* let Jane get close on that ugly water tank of hers."

By now Bill had daubed witch hazel into his cuts and scrapes. Matt called all the men into a tight circle for Hickok's final instructions.

"Boys, from here on out we're officially a trail drive. You'll have to listen close to me and Matt, and learn quick, because I'll guarantee you we don't have much room for mistakes. Never mind how small this herd might seem. We ain't trained drovers, so it'll seem plenty big to us."

Bill's eyes stayed in motion as he spoke, missing nothing. The next attempt on his life could come in an instant.

"Nights are especially dangerous on a cattle drive, because that's when the cows are most likely to spook and stampede. So night discipline must be strictly enforced, Matt, including punishments if you need 'em. Every swinging dick, no matter what your job, has to avoid *any* sudden or loud noise. After dark, I've known of a horse's sneeze scattering a herd to hell and gone."

Corporal Langford passed, walking his big seventeen-hand sorrel, keeping the herd bunched as ordered. Bill nodded in his direction.

"What Abel's doing right now is called close-herding or guarding the herd. It's to be done whenever the herd is bedded down for the night. Two riders all night long, slow and easy, one clockwise, one counterclockwise. And while you're riding, you *sing* to the beeves."

"Sing to 'em?" one of the men piped up. "Sergeant Jones, that's *your* line! That man sings all night long anyhow, Wild Bill. Knows all them spiritual songs."

"That's the ticket," Bill agreed. "Slow, easy, soothing tunes like 'Swing Low, Sweet Chariot.' None of this 'Jim Crack Corn' or 'Yankee Doodle Dandy' to stir up the cattle. Night riders remember—you're not only the first line of defense if something spooks the herd, you're camp security, too. Treat this like any other military guard duty."

Just then, Calamity Jane's camel, Ignatius, loosed a raucous bray that made donkeys sound like crooners. Luckily, Josh noticed, they were staying far enough back to avoid spooking cattle or horses.

"As for actually moving the herd," Bill resumed.

"The more they're allowed to spread out and scatter, the more likely they are to sull on you, to start fighting. Especially crossing through good graze. So we'll want to keep them tight-bunched, with the lead bulls always front and center."

He paused so his next point would be underscored.

"The key to close-herding is good swing men, or flank riders. A cow naturally breaks from the main gather by charging right or left, not by slowing down. So the best riders, with the quickest, most agile horses, are needed on the flanks whenever the herd is moving."

Wild Bill paused, wondering if he should mention river crossings yet. But their first ford wasn't until they hit the Colorado River, still days to the north. Best to wait, he decided—they had enough to learn as it was.

"One last thing for now," Bill wrapped it, "is what to do if the herd breaks and stampedes. Once they start running, there ain't no brakes on 'em. So there's only one way to regain control: We have to throw 'em into a mill."

Hickok traced circles in the air with his right index finger. "We turn 'em in a circle and then just let 'em run it out."

Joshua, who had at least *read* about cattle drives, knew that Wild Bill hadn't even touched on such constant dangers as rattlesnakes, flash floods, and dehydration in the water-scarce areas. Cattle were also susceptible to "the scours," a form of dysentery that could cost them half their weight.

Instead of mentioning all that, he simply said, "That's it for now. Matt, make the job assignments, and then we're moving out. I'll be riding out ahead to take up the point. We get back to your camp near San Antone, we'll bed down the herd, then have our new cook shake us up some eatins."

However, another problem cropped up—a homely problem wearing a John B. Stetson and toting a Smith & Wesson with a twelve-inch barrel. Nobody had seen Jane sneaking up on them. She'd left Ignatius behind on a tether.

A few of the men sniggered at the lecherous glance she aimed at Joshua. "Bill tells me you're ridin' drag, you cute little son-of-a-buck," she told the blushing youth. "You can dip your wick anytime you want—I'll be close by."

Hickok didn't escape in time either.

"Wild Bill!" she roared out. "Dadgarnit, I just saved your handsome hide. Don't I at least get to have a snort with the famous man?"

She held high a bottle of Doyle's Hop Bitters, "the invalid's friend and hope." The popular patent medicine was worthless as a curative, but got you so drunk you didn't care anyway.

Bill knew he was trapped by his own good range manners. He couldn't refuse to drink with Jane after what she'd done. But this woman was death-to-the-devil once she pulled a cork.

"I'm watching my drinking now, Bill," she assured him when she saw the wary glint in his eyes. "I've taken a page from Buffalo Bill Cody's book. That gentleman has limited himself to one glass of bourbon a day, and he sticks to his limit."

Every man present—except Bill and Josh, who knew her too well—burst into appreciative laughter when Jane reached into the saddle pannier draped over her shoulder and produced a one-quart glass!

"You men!" Matt shouted, fighting to keep a straight face himself. "You heard Wild Bill's orders. Stop gawking like chawbacons and move that herd!"

"The best way to take down a gun slick like Hickok," Harding Ott said, "is not by challenging his strengths. It's best to get at him by way of his weaknesses. And for J. B. Hickok, that means poker and beautiful women. You, Fel, are a combination of both."

Felicity "Fel" Parker acknowledged the compliment with a gracious bowing of her head. She was a chestnut-haired beauty with smoke-colored eyes and a come-hither smile.

"Isn't this a rather grandiose scheme you're hatching?" Fel challenged him. "I mean, it's one thing to bully some Indians into moving so you can use their land."

"Bully? That's hard, Fel," he protested. "I have a lease, sworn and signed by their tribal representative."

Fel's grin revealed pretty little teeth like polished pearls. "Harding, an *X* made by your paid lackey may get challenged in court."

"In court?" Ott laughed, amused at his former partner's naïveté concerning Indians. "Darling, not one case tried in a white man's court has gone the red man's way. It's like trying to prosecute a white man for lynching a black in the South."

Fel said nothing to this, demurely fanning her face with a palmetto fan. Ott had taken her to his office in Ogallala, which was far more prosperous looking than his hovel outside of town—which he only kept to hide Woman Dress from his wealthy clients. His "falderol house," as Olney Lucas called it.

"Wild Bill Hickok," Fel said a moment later, "does not share in the red man's current bad luck. In fact, common men *and* royalty all touch him for luck. That man escaped from the Confederate Army three times, once only minutes before he was to be executed. You see, Harding, *that's* what is so grandiose of you. Thinking you, of all men, can kill him."

"Oh, I probably can't," he conceded. "But you can."

"So what if I could? Why *should* I? Even if I could get away with it, why would I want to? I believe in live and let live. The man is so handsome, women leave convents to chase him. And I'm told he's an extraordinarily . . . spirited lover. What would be my incentive to kill a robust stallion like him?"

Ott knew Felicity well, and had expected all of

this. He countered her objections immediately.

"How about twenty-five thousand dollars?" he asked her. "Is that incentive enough?"

"My goodness! That figure does give the heart a jupe," she admitted.

It was a staggering sum when Fel considered how the average Jack supported a family on about $350 yearly.

"You could invest it," Ott tantalized her, "and live comfortably in Paris on the interest alone. Never have to work another shill game."

Fel gave all this careful consideration. Upon receiving Ott's urgent telegram, she had boarded the next eastbound train from Cheyenne. It was a straight hop to Ogallala, little more than a half-day's trip.

Only an offer from her former partner could have enticed her to leave Cheyenne right now. Fel ran that town's only "pleasure emporium for cowboys," a lucrative business. But the winds of change were blowing.

"Maybe your telegram was well-timed," Fel finally replied. "Right now I'm taking in more gold cartwheels than the local Wells Fargo. But a group of blue-nosed temperance biddies are getting up a drive to run me out—you know, cleansing Babylon of the whore and all that."

Ott's lips creased in a mirthless smile. "Ahh yes, the Outraged Citizens. Remember Albany?"

Oh Lord, *did* she! Remembered it with a little shudder as she recalled the close call. Back east, she and Harding had specialized in the "cuckold" con. Felicity would use her looks and polished charm to seduce wealthy married men into "compromising positions," literally, and then blackmail them when her "outraged spouse" caught them in flagrante delicto.

But they played their game one time too often, and were exposed in New York, where they were chased out of Albany by a tar-and-feather mob.

Fel shook off this unpleasant reverie and raised her eyes toward an artist's representation mounted on the wall behind Ott's desk.

"So that's your dream city, huh?" she asked him.

The idyllic projection was labeled "Commerce Bluffs." It showed a thriving mercantile city hugging the bank of the South Platte, surrounded by fields of wheat.

"It's not *my* dream," he corrected her. "In fact, I seriously doubt the city will ever materialize. But as long as my foreign investors *believe* it will, the money keeps rolling in."

"Let me guess," Fel took over. "Right now those investors are balking because they aren't sure the Indians *will* move well south of the river?"

He looked impressed. "Exactly. You've put the ax right on the helve."

Ott turned around in his chair to look at the handsome sketch of Commerce Bluffs. "If those Indians stay put, all of my big plans are mental vapors. And with a beef herd arriving, they *will* stay put."

"Therefore, you want me to kill Wild Bill Hickok?"

Ott nodded. But he didn't bother to tell her that she was only insurance against a failure by the Lucas boys. And he had faith in their dark talents at killing. Even now they were racing south to intercept the herd. If Olney and Jip came through for him, Fel was just out of luck.

"Have you worked it out?" she pressed. "How my trail will cross his, and all the details?"

"From soup to nuts," he assured her. "Hickok won't suspect a thing."

"Well, why not do it?" she finally consented. "The money is fine, and Hickok is quite alluring. This could be my most enjoyable piece of work yet."

A cautionary note took over Ott's tone. "You must be careful not to find him *too* 'alluring.' If you foolishly fall in love with him, you'll regret it. The only woman he's faithful to is the queen in a poker deck."

Fel laughed, a charming, feminine laugh just dripping charm and grace. "Fall in love with him. So what if I do? Does the female spider hesitate to kill her mate once she's had her use of him?"

Fel's slim white hand produced a little alligator jewel case from the folds of her ostrich-feather boa. Ott smiled in satisfaction when she snapped the case open and he saw the .38-caliber derringer made by Brasher of London—the famous "muff gun" for ladies, tiny yet deadly at point-blank range.

"Harding, it's not the money that motivates

me," she assured him. "It's the *amount*. For twenty-five thousand dollars, I'd shoot Saint Peter at the Pearly Gates. Now tell me more about this foolproof scheme of yours."

Chapter Seven

The first three days on the trail were uneventful and remarkably easy—too easy, Hickok fretted, watching how the others reacted.

The land varied little except near water: flat or rolling grassland, but sparse and semiarid, dotted with juniper, sage, and cactus. Gnarled cottonwoods appeared near the rivers. They made between fifteen and twenty miles all three days—an excellent pace, especially considering that time was set aside each day so the herd could graze.

Joshua's growing cockiness, as this easy routine emerged, was typical of the rest. True, the kid had discovered that riding drag behind cattle meant literally eating their dust. But the herd had been remarkably tractable and well-behaved, so far. Now Josh and the rest were all getting salty and smug, sure they'd mastered the cowboy's craft.

"Why, hell!" Josh called out during supper on that third night. "I'd walk a mile to kick an old sheep in the side!"

The rest, except for Matt, cheered, feeling like full-fledged cowhands. But Wild Bill knew better. Pushing beeves under excellent conditions was no great challenge. These men had no idea, however, just how quickly things could go to hell. Or that their big, untrained horses would not be adequate to face real trouble.

"Colorado River's coming up tomorrow," Wild Bill informed Matt and Joshua. The three men had just rinsed their metal plates in the wreck pan, a big roaster filled with soapy water that Rob Meadows had set on the tailgate of the buckboard.

"Let 'er rip," Josh boasted. "Hickok's Misfits can whip anything."

Josh would not be able to file his next dispatch until the trail bypassed Fort Worth, the next telegraph office. But it was already half written, and he had deliberately alluded to himself as "one of Hickok's misfits on the trail." He knew editors well—that phrase would appear in the headlines, too.

"We'll see how feisty you are after we cross a river or two," Hickok told him. "And after we cross all the rivers in Texas, there's plenty more. The Red River, the Washita, the Canadian, the North Canadian, the Cimarron, the Salt Fork, the Arkansas, the Little Arkansas. Neither bridge nor ferry at any of 'em—not for cattle, anyhow."

By now Josh looked subdued, if not daunted.

"Cimarron," he repeated, recalling his Spanish. "That means 'wild.' "

"They can all be wild," Bill assured him. "Even the quiet ones hide quicksand or snakes. But we should be all right tomorrow. Assuming this rainstorm I feel coming on don't turn out to be a gully-washer."

Bill turned to Matt. "I found a good place where some sandy shoals should make for a shallow, slow current."

"Exactly how should we move 'em across?" Matt asked practically. "Let 'em come up on the water easy and just coax 'em after they drink?"

Bill shook his head. "Hell no! You got it hindside foremost. They drink on this side, they'll get loggy and go under before they get across. The big trick is to close-herd 'em, bunch 'em tight as ticks before the river. Then we push 'em fast toward the water. That forces the lead animals to take the plunge. The rest will follow. They can drink when they get over."

"Man, I got a lot to learn," Matt conceded.

"Walk, trot, canter, then gallop," Bill replied. "Take it a step at a time, son, you'll get up to speed."

Hickok slid a half-smoked cheroot from his fob pocket and borrowed a glowing ember from the campfire to light it.

He looks worn out, Josh thought, and why shouldn't he? On a trail drive, the work went on "from can to can't." The real clock had ceased to matter, for every man measured out his toil in sweat, not hours. And no man's day was longer than the scout's.

Each morning, fortified with black coffee strong enough to float a horseshoe, Hickok rode out alone. It was his critical job to range ahead and locate adequate grass—otherwise "the creeps" would soon set in, the general weakness of cattle brought on by starvation.

Wild Bill had once watched an entire herd lost to the creeps farther west, on the Goodnight-Loving Trail. Against Bill's advice, the rancher left too late in the season, with all the grass already eaten. The cows quickly deteriorated to hide-covered skeletons, their sharp pelvic bones actually lancing their hides. Their spines bowed, and all they could muster were small, weak steps. Turkey buzzards started circling even before the first longhorns dropped dead.

Maybe they're only stupid cows, Wild Bill told himself as he stabbed a bootjack into his heel, tugging off his boots. But I'm damned if they'll starve on my watch.

"Poker game making up, Wild Bill!" called out Big Swede, the cook's assistant, from the other side of the fire. "Civilian money is good, too."

Hickok immediately perked up. "Be there in two shakes, boys," he replied.

At night, the men who weren't on night duty or dead tired amused themselves at card games, mostly poker and monte. Although Bill never missed these games, he was a true gentleman and refused to fleece enlisted men. Thus, the pots remained frustratingly low.

"You're champing at the bit for a high-stakes game, are'n'cha?" Josh said.

"This penny-ante stuff is tame," Bill conceded. "It's like drinking watered-down liquor."

"Well, Jane's got money to burn," Josh said with a poker face. "I saw her bankroll."

Bill's eyebrows rose. "That a fact? Hmm . . . gold shiners?"

"Naw, eastern money," Josh replied, meaning paper banknotes. "That's how the Army pays."

"It all spends," Bill said thoughtfully. "But Jane's horny as a brass band."

"I'll tell the world," Josh affirmed. "Why do you think she showed me the money?"

Matt grinned. "You don't mean she . . . ?"

Josh flushed. "Offered to pay by the hour, even."

"Huh! You better get her down to minutes," Wild Bill suggested.

Josh ignored that. "I'm the one has to stay close to her," he complained bitterly.

He was glad the other two couldn't see him blushing, thanks to the burnished-orange glow of the sawing flames. Some of the things Jane called out to him would make a dead man blush. *C'mon back here, you handsome young buck, and give Janey a little scratch where she itches.*

"So far," Bill pointed out gratefully, "she's been good about following well back so's not to spook the herd."

Josh could confirm this. Jane stayed just back

from the dust cloud that choked him all day. But just like Bill, she too went off on her little scouting missions each day. Protecting Bill, as usual.

Before he went to join the card game, Bill asked Matt: "How the men doing? They settling into the watches all right?"

Matt nodded. "They wouldn't be soldiers if there wasn't some bitching and griping. The only one who's really miserable is Private Mosley."

"It's a miserable job," Bill conceded. "Lowest on a cattle drive. That's what he gets for being popular with horses."

John "Johnny Reb" Mosley was a southern lad who was particularly good at gentling and controlling horses. Bill had made him horse wrangler, in charge of caring for the entire remuda. The twenty Cavalry remounts had been augmented by five more cow ponies purchased from Dolph Reynolds.

"On the other hand," Matt added, "Rob Meadows has taken to it like a duck to water. Having a good cook like him along sure makes a difference, Wild Bill. Hell, his trail fare is better than we get in garrison."

It was true. What that man could do with a handful of wild onions or coriander was amazing. The meals were simple but well prepared from fresh-butchered beef. Chipped beef over biscuits for the morning meal, beef and beans in the evening. No matter how early Bill woke up each morning, Meadows was already at work, cutting out several pans of sourdough biscuits.

"I do wish I'd thought about chaps," Matt admitted. "A couple of the men have scraped their legs pretty raw."

"I forgot, too," Hickok said. "But we'll be okay once we're north of the Brazos—cactus thins out then."

Josh listened with a reporter's ear, for he meant to capture the details of this trail drive that dime novels glossed over. Matt was green, but the young officer was a natural leader of men, as was Hickok. With two steady men like them at the helm, no wonder an efficient routine had been quickly established for the trail.

Despite his aching, dust-swollen eyes and sore tailbone, Joshua was actually enjoying this real-life western adventure. The nights especially, when the furnace heat of day rapidly cooled to a bracing chill. Sage crackled under the hooves of the grazing herd, releasing its fresh aroma.

But now, as Josh peered into that shadowy unknown beyond the comforting fire, guilt lanced him deep. When would the next bounty hunter or glory seeker try to send Wild Bill under?

He wanted to help, but he couldn't. Wild Bill was out on point—he was back in the drag slot. The entire cattle drive separated them.

"Sweet dreams, fellas," Wild Bill told them as he fished a bottle of Old Taylor from a saddlebag. "Think I'll play a little five-card before I get my beauty rest."

*　　*　　*

Wild Bill rolled up in his blankets well before midnight, worried about the weather as he drifted off to sleep. That new year had begun with a January chinook, a warming wind from the southwest. He knew that was a portent of bad weather to come.

Sure enough, the first dark thunderheads were rolling over the horizon even as Bill woke up at sunrise.

Otis Jones rode slowly by, singing quietly to the still-resting herd. The cattle seemed to quiet instantly at the sound of his basso profundo voice singing old spirituals, and so did the men. He was so calming to the herd, in fact, that Bill told Matt to take Otis off day duty so he could ride longer at night.

"Gonna rain like the dickens, Mr. Hickok," Otis called over softly, seeing Bill up and buckling on his shell belt.

"I see that, Otis. How long you think it might hold off?"

"Middle morning, at the latest."

Bill nodded. "That's how I make it, too. About the same time we'll reach the Colorado."

"Should we hold off crossing till after the rain?"

"The problem with the Colorado," Bill replied, "is that it floods quick but recedes slow. Usually the grass along the banks grows tall enough to shine your boots when you ride through it. But now there's no bed grass there, earlier herds have taken it off. We might have to wait a week for that river to settle."

"So we best move while the gate is open," Otis

concluded. "Push the herd hard and get 'em over."

"The way you say. Roust out Lieutenant Carlson and the rest, and tell Meadows to secure his kitchen. We're skipping breakfast until after we cross that river."

Bill started to turn away, but then added: "Hey, also tell Meadows to lash down the supplies so we can float the buckboard over on guide ropes. No ferry here."

"Yessir!"

Thus began a desperate race against time and the elements. By the time flank riders were in place, yipping the herd up and into motion, the first stuttering rumble of thunder rolled across the land.

Of all the times for the herd to start rebelling, they picked this gray, storm-pregnant morning. The swing men couldn't hold them. Something wild in the air communicated itself to them. Wild Bill and Matt were both forced to serve as extra outriders, constantly hazing rebellious cattle back into the main gather.

Not every steer went back placidly, either. Their horns were deadly, and more than one attempted to gore the men's horses. Bill trusted Fire-away's reflexes, and the savvy roan ducked death time after time.

Even Calamity Jane saw the drama unfolding and joined the fray. Any cattle that eluded Joshua at the rear were literally frightened back up into the main gather when she rushed them on Ignatius, screeching Cheyenne war cries while the camel brayed raucously.

About a half-mile from the Colorado River, the heavens opened up on them. Gray, driving sheets of rain pounded down with such fury, it stung the men's skin like buckshot. They pulled on their bright yellow slickers. Teeth gritted against it, they drove on.

Wild Bill, who rarely spurred any horse, poked his rowels into Fire-away's flanks, sending the roan toward the river in a streak. Bill had to check the water level quick—if the river had risen too much, the herd would have to be turned, and damn soon.

He topped a low bluff and saw the river in front of him, on the rise but not too high—just yet. However, the rain still fell in torrents, and the river grew more turbulent with each passing minute.

It's got to be done, Wild Bill decided. Take one big risk now, or face lingering starvation as the herd waited for it to recede.

He wheeled his horse and raced back to join the others.

"Bunch 'em up!" he shouted. "I mean tight, lads! They'll balk in this rain, but we've *got* to drive 'em across now! C'mon, damnit, tighten it up! Nose to tail, cluster 'em!"

All the men knew their orders. Two men would plunge their horses into the river even before the herd—they had to cross first to hold the cattle. The rest of the men would literally shove all the cattle, if need be, into the river. Then all of them, astride their horses, would take the plunge to guide the cows straight across.

Straight was the key. The biggest danger was that the herd might turn downstream in the current, thus exhausting themselves and drowning.

But they soon had another problem: Despite the big push, the herd had somehow sulled on the sagebrush flats near the river. Simply come to a complete stop, refusing to be driven.

Yipping at them, whacking them, even firing gunshots—nothing could force the lead bulls into the ever-rising, swirling currents.

"Joshua!" Bill sang out. "Hustle back and tell Jane to charge the herd on Ignatius!"

It worked. Calamity Jane, shucking out her short iron and firing rounds into the air, rode right up onto the rear of the herd, terrifying them. As they rammed forward, the lead longhorns were simply pushed into the river. They splashed in, bawling in protest, whipping the water to spray.

Those who had never seen cattle swim assumed the animals were drowning. The longhorns sank deep, only their tilted heads above water—and then, only nostrils, eyes, horns.

"Follow me, boys!" Wild Bill roared out above the sheeting rain. "Copy what I do! *Don't* drift past that gravel bank on the left—there's a quicksand bank."

Joshua, recording the sight for millions of readers, stood there soaking wet, watching in awe. Fire-away plunged bravely in, and as soon as the gelding was over his head, Bill slid off to ease the load. He simply grabbed the horse's tail as a tow-rope.

The others followed suit. Unexpected currents caught at some of the cattle, and men had to crowd them back into line.

"C'mon, boy!" Joshua urged his coyote dun, "let's take a bath!"

They plunged into the rain-swollen river just as Wild Bill and his horse reached midstream. Joshua shuddered as the cold river water shocked him breathless.

Moments later, another cold shock numbed him. Josh watched a man with a rifle step out from behind a cottonwood, drawing a bead on Hickok!

Chapter Eight

A spur line of the Atchison, Topeka, and Santa Fe Railroad took Jip, Olney, and their horses south to Fort Belknap on the Brazos River in north central Texas. From there they dusted their hocks south at a breakneck pace, finally intercepting the cattle drive as it approached the Colorado.

They were careful to keep a low line of hills between themselves and the two men sent over first to hold the cattle. The Lucas boys tethered their horses so they'd be out of sight from the south bank of the river, yet close enough for a quick get-away. Then, even as the rain began to pound down on them, they took up positions in the scrub cottonwood and mesquite crowding the north bank.

"River's rising," Olney fretted, sheltering as best he could against a cottonwood. "They don't get here damn soon, they'll have to wait. Christ! Lookit!"

The two brothers watched a lone rider on a handsome roan top the distant bluff.

"It's Hickok," Olney gloated. "Sure as cats fighting! See that womanish long hair? He's come to check on the river."

Olney slid a handsome Berdan breech-loading rifle from its buckskin sheath. The bolt-action weapon was chambered for .42-caliber center-fire cartridges.

"That skirt-chasing bastard comes close enough," he vowed, "I'll plug him now."

Olney longed to get this job over with. The worst thing about these tail jobs was the grub. Yesterday he had shot and dressed out a pronghorn buck. The meat was tough, but it was better than Jip's damned jackrabbit stew.

But Hickok didn't give the chance to finish it quick. He abruptly wheeled his mount and galloped back, the roan's hooves tossing divots of mud high into the air.

"They're going to cross it now," Olney gloated. "Elsewise he wouldn't be rushing back like that."

Thus the Lucas boys had watched it all unfold as the drive reached the river. Olney shook his brother's arm when the entire herd was in the river.

"Look, yonder comes Hickok," Olney said above the steady hiss of rain. "Yeah-boy! This could work out perfect. Way the river's on a rise? If I plug the bastard midstream, his body'll wash down to that elbow bend, maybe tangle in that big sawyer with the brush and driftwood. We'll lop off his pretty head and go collect our bounty."

Jip, watching Hickok and his horse guide the cattle even while swimming, seemed less confident.

"Ain't this a helluva risk, Olney? That's Hickok, not some unarmed Injun."

Olney was already easing out from behind cover for a better shot. "Sure it's a risk. You can't make an omelet, big brother, without breaking some eggs."

Jip's doltish face crumpled in confusion. "I don't know how to make no omelets."

Olney, who was always patient with his slow-witted brother, said gently: "Shh—shush it now. There's my target."

Amid that crescendo of storm and bawling cattle and shouting men, Wild Bill never even heard a weapon detonate. And with cattle whipping the river to froth, he didn't notice the first bullets raising columns of water.

However, he instantly recognized the angry-hornet sound when a bullet passed within a cat's whisker of one ear!

He looked up at the far bank and saw the rain-hazy shape of a man, shooting at him from the kneeling offhand position. And with each yard Bill floated closer, he made the shot easier.

He had already lashed his gunbelt to his saddle horn to keep it above water. His .44s were thus out of reach. But Bill managed to tug his Winchester '72 from its boot.

However, it was no child's task to stay afloat. With one hand he held Fire-away's tail, while aiming and firing a rifle with the other—all while ducking lead at the same time.

Just when he had a shaky, one-armed bead on his man, a swirling eddy sucked him in, and Bill started choking. A bullet punched into his saddle fender; another traced a white-hot tickle when it grazed his left temple.

That eddy lifted him for a moment; Hickok fired, missed, levered, and fired again. This time, before the river smacked him back down, Bill saw his second shot blow the man's floppy hat off his head. Damn, thought Bill, bucked my aim by a hair. But that near miss was enough to send the ambusher scurrying back behind the trees.

The scene on the north bank, when Bill finally gained it, was at sixes and sevens. The two soldiers sent to hold the cattle had done their inept best. But in this downpour, their big Army horses kept stumbling on the cuts, and perhaps a hundred beeves had scattered broadcast.

When the herd had finally been bunched and the rain was dwindling off, Wild Bill and Josh loped their horses out across the flats, looking for sign. But the bad weather had wiped out any tracks as quickly as they were made.

They returned to the river. By now the buckboard had been towed safely across, but one wheel had been shattered on the rocks.

"Big Swede and Johnny Reb are fixing it now," Matt reported. "Should be ready to roll in about an hour."

"No big hurry anyway," Wild Bill assured him. "After that swim, the herd needs to rest and graze. And the men missed breakfast. They all make it across?"

Matt nodded. "One man lost his rifle, but I had a replacement for him. Speaking of rifles—any sign of whoever shot at you?"

Wild Bill shook his head, three fingertips feeling the tender spot where he'd been creased.

"They never leave their calling cards," he quipped wryly. "What gripes my ass," he added, glowering at Joshua, "is that when some lowlife finally *does* drill me in the back, the press will make a damned hero out of him."

"Heroes, villains, and fools," Josh admitted. "It's all we write about."

Rain had brought out hordes of ravenous mosquitoes, some half as big as a man's thumb. Bill told Meadows to use up the damp wood in the cooney, the sling underneath the buckboard. Damp wood smoked when tossed on a fire, and it chased off some of the skeeters.

The men stripped out of their sopping clothing and spread it out to dry. During a meal of beef and biscuits, Joshua asked Bill: "Did Pinkerton say who killed Chief White Bear?"

Although Pinkerton had slinked out of town without facing Hickok, he'd left a letter behind about this latest case.

Bill shook his head. "Nope. But before they could even put the chief on his funeral scaffold, there's a fellow named Harding Ott who gets the Sioux to 'lease' the best part of the rez to him. Now, ain't that providential?"

"Is it legal? I mean, to lease government land from federal wards?"

Bill snorted. "No, it ain't legal. But neither is squatting on federal land. Yet that's how most of the rich men out west got their start. Know what else?"

"What?"

"Taking potshots at *me* ain't legal either, kid, but thanks to your profession, it's becoming a national pastime. Don't forget—the 'law' is way the hell back east. There ain't but a few thousand troops west of the Mississippi, and even fewer lawmen."

Bill stared Josh straight in the eye and added: "Men do what they need to out here, the law be damned."

All things considered, Wild Bill decided that their first river crossing had gone pretty well, even with the ambush.

But there were tougher fords up ahead, including "Big Red" and another river that almost drowned him back in '67, the cantankerous Arkansas.

At first Hickok had assumed this latest attempt on his life was just random bounty hunting. But

Joshua's question, about who killed Chief White Bear, set Bill to pondering.

If this Harding Ott fellow was willing to kill Indian leaders, willing to risk government intervention by swindling red men out of their land, would he just sit idly by while Hickok ruined all of his plans? Or might he send paid killers ahead to stop the cattle drive?

"I spoze it don't really matter," Wild Bill concluded philosophically, after talking it over with Joshua early next morning. "Reward hunters, paid killers—hell, they're just two sides of the same coin. They all mean to plant me."

Bill spat out the mouthful of coffee he'd just tried to swallow. "Well, God kiss me! Damn, Rob!" he called over to the cook. "You could cut a plug off this so-called coffee!"

"'At's right," Private Meadows fired back. "What you don't drink now you can chew later! You complaining, Wild Bill?" he demanded.

"No, sir," Bill replied meekly, for even the mighty Hickok knew the sacred law of the trail: Any man who criticizes the cooking must take over the job.

The rest of the men were preparing to move out. The herd was well rested and grazed, and Wild Bill had already scouted ahead yesterday to locate tonight's bed ground.

"Calamity Jane visit you last night in your bedroll?" Hickok roweled Josh.

"I been sleeping under the buckboard," the reporter confessed. "You best look out too, Bill. *You're* the gent she's in love with."

"I hadn't noticed," Bill shot back sarcastically.

He stood up and, removing each gun in turn, palmed the wheels to check his loads.

"I'm just lucky," he told the kid, "that Jane gets drunk every night and sleeps like a winter bear."

"Bill?"

"Mmm?"

"How come you still navigate by the stars? Matt's got a compass. Besides, we're following a cattle trail, so what's the difference?"

Joshua was alluding to the way that, each night, Bill had the men line the tongue of the buckboard up with the polestar to hold true north.

"Once the sun goes down," Hickok reminded him, "we need a quick point of reference in case we lose the herd and have to ride out after them in a hurry. Not every man has got a compass, and besides, they ain't always reliable during storms and such."

"Oh. But what if clouds obscure the North Star?"

"Then you can usually use the wind as your compass. Around here, it almost always blows from the southwest at night."

That's how he survives, Josh admired. It wasn't Bill's highly fabled "luck." Luck governed him only at the poker table—and sometimes when Jane showed up at the eleventh hour.

In truth it was sound trail craft, which Bill Hickok had learned from the likes of Kit Carson,

Charles Bent, General Jim Lane, and other masters of frontier survival.

"Ready to move 'em out, Wild Bill!" Matt reported from the saddle. "All the riders are posted except the drag, Joshua. Look lively, wordsmith!"

The kid frowned, but stoically tied a bandanna over the lower half of his face to cut the dust. He could see Calamity Jane stirring back behind them near the river. She caught him watching her and began to unbutton her shirt with one hand, the other beckoning to him. He felt a shudder move down his spine.

"Back to the salt mines," he muttered, grabbing leather and trotting his coyote dun back toward the rear of the herd. He veered wide, however, of the bathing woman.

Bill cut Fire-away out from the string and threw on a blanket and pad, then the saddle, cinching the girth tight. The gelding took the bit eagerly, ready to ride again.

While Matt and his military cowboys yipped the herd into motion, Bill loped his mount easily out across the green tableland stretching away from the river. He let the entire vista "come up to his eye" rather than try to concentrate on small sections of it.

Thus he first caught a slight motion in the tail of his right eye—a person on foot, approaching from the parched hills to the east. He monitored the figure's progress as he continued riding north, letting Fire-away set his own pace.

Bill knew the herd would no longer make its

rapid progress of the first few days. The Chisholm Trail, between the Colorado and the Brazos, was often sandy and rocky, with washouts that had to be detoured. He was also worried about adequate water. The Brazos was still four or five days away.

And then, of course, he also had to keep a weather eye out for would-be assassins—at which thought Bill reined in, watching the figure approaching from the east.

He slid the brass binoculars from his saddle pocket and focused in on the solitary hiker.

"Well, I'll be hog-tied and ear-marked," Hickok said out loud to his horse. "This trail just took an interesting turn, old campaigner."

Bill marveled at the young woman's ostrich-feather boa, the gay, beribboned hat, the fancy, velvet-trimmed traveling outfit. But mostly he focused on that stunning, oval-shaped face with its pronounced cheekbones and heart-shaped lips.

She carried a valise, switching it from arm to arm to ease the weight. Bill tossed the reins over Fire-away's head, letting them dangle, and the well-trained horse came to a halt. Neither hobbles nor tether were required when the reins dangled.

Wild Bill swung down and slid a cheroot from his shirt pocket, skinning back the paper wrapper as he watched the woman trudge closer.

"Sir!" she hailed him in a voice like violins lifting. "Did an angel send you to help me?"

Bill stuck the cigar in his teeth and lit it, then folded his arms over his chest, watching her.

"We haven't discussed it," he confessed in his

mild, easy way as she hauled up before him. "Might I ask why you're riding shank's mare out here in the middle of nothing, Miss . . . ?"

"Jackson. Sandra Jackson. From the sublime to the ridiculous is but a step," she assured him. She set the valise down, then lifted her right foot to massage the instep. "Or, in my case—ouch!— many steps."

Bill took in her smoky gray eyes shaped like nutshells, the skin like flawless ivory. Her smile was restive, like a woman with secret thoughts of a naughty color.

"You seem to have held up quite well, Miss Jackson," Bill told her.

"That," she said coquettishly, "is a left-handed compliment if I've ever heard one! Why not just tell me I'm not *too* ugly?"

Bill laughed, basking in the presence of an accomplished flirt.

"No man in his right mind would leave you behind," he said. "So tell me—did you do the leaving?"

"I'm running from a man," she confessed. "But it's not like you're thinking, Mister . . . ?"

"Hickok. J. B. Hickok."

"As in—Wild Bill Hickok?"

"You look surprised. But I'm right where I belong," Hickok assured her. "In the *wild*. You, madam, are the one who's out of her element. I'd guess, from that lovely accent, that you're from the Deep South? Perhaps Mississippi?"

"Lake Charles, Louisiana," she corrected him.

"On my way to Wichita, Kansas, to visit my ailing father."

Her story was straightforward and quite believable, given the dearth of law officers out here. The stagecoach she was riding was robbed in the bayou country of east Texas, Sandra reported. She said one of the bandits took a liking to her—also quite believable—and kidnapped her. She later escaped when they camped to sleep.

Believable, all right, if you didn't think about it much. But Bill had been a law officer too many years, and he immediately noted the discrepancies. For one thing, this gal did not show the harried look of someone who'd just been through hell.

Not that Bill cared all that much *if* she was lying—only *why*. Many folks came west to lose their old baggage, and sometimes the lies they told were harmless enough.

"So you decided to hike across Texas until you hooked up with a cattle drive, that it?"

"My first choice would be a town. But a . . . gallant gentleman will do," she assured him, batting kohl-darkened lashes. "I couldn't exactly stop by the livery and rent a rig, now could I?"

"Hardly," Bill agreed, watching her with thoughtful interest. "Well, madam, I can't offer you rapid or comfortable transit. But the drive I'm with happens to be going right past Wichita."

"What a happy coincidence!"

His strong white teeth flashed under his mustache when he smiled. "Ain't it, though?" he replied, more polite than ironic, but just barely.

Bill took the valise from her and lashed it to his saddle with a rawhide whang.

"It's a tight saddle," Hickok warned her as he lifted Sandra into it, noticing how light and trim the beauty was. "But I think we can both squeeze in."

"I'm not a good rider," she apologized. "Forgive me if I hold you too tight."

"I'm trained for the tough jobs," he joked.

But as he stepped up into leather himself, Hickok couldn't prevent an unwelcome thought.

He had just violated one of his cardinal rules of survival: He was leaving his back vulnerable to a stranger.

Chapter Nine

It was universally known that Wild Bill Hickok had a sixth sense reserved for locating beautiful women. But no one in Lieutenant Matt Carlson's cattle detail expected the frontiersman to locate one out *here*, smack in the middle of the endless Texas prairie.

By the time Wild Bill returned, with his pretty passenger hugging her ample bodice against him, Matt had halted the herd for the midday graze. Two men were pitching a game of horseshoes, two more arm wrestling for bettors, when someone called out: "Eyes right, boys! Wild Bill must have run his traps—look what he's caught!"

"Hey, Wild Bill!" Big Swede sang out. "Next time you ride out? Bring me back one, too!"

Whistles and cheers greeted this remark.

"You men keep a civil tongue in your heads!"

Matt barked out. However, he, too, couldn't stop staring at the tantalizing glimpse of shapely calf where the woman's skirt had ridden up.

Bill grinned, enjoying it immensely. Against the grimly masculine backdrop of a trail camp, the beauty behind him stood out like a brass spittoon in a funeral parlor.

Sandra Jackson did not, however, give the men a chance to intimidate her.

"How do you know, fella," she challenged Swede boldly, "that Bill *didn't* bring me back for you? Just 'cause I'm squeezed against him doesn't mean I live in his hip pocket!"

All the men cheered at this, and Swede blushed to the tip of his nose.

"Now, Swede here is a married man, ma'am," Abel Langford piped up. "And though I've only one good eye, it sure likes what it sees. You know, Lieutenant Carlson can, by law, perform weddings."

By now Wild Bill had handed his passenger down from her perch. She smoothed her skirt with both hands, evidently unperturbed by the intense scrutiny she was receiving.

"I'm sure Lieutenant Carlson is a very capable officer," she said sweetly. "And I hope you all obey him like good boys. Just one question: Are you cowboys or soldiers?"

"Whichever you was hopin' for, dumplin'," Johnny Reb assured her in his syrupy drawl, and the men all cheered that, too.

Bill kept his face straight with an effort. "Miss

Jackson here," he explained succinctly, "has escaped from abductors. She wonders if we'd be willing to escort her north to Wichita."

"Do mad dogs howl at the moon?" Rob Meadows responded, and every man voted with him in one voice.

"You can sleep in my tent, ma'am," Matt volunteered, missing the risqué hint of his remark.

"Why, Lieutenant—you military men *are* fast," she teased him.

"Uh, I muh—meant for *your* use only, of course," he clarified. "It's just a one-person pup tent."

Bill had to choke back a laugh at this contretemps.

"The hell you grinning at, kid?" he challenged Joshua. "At least Matt doesn't color up like a schoolgirl."

Naturally Joshua blushed at this, and blushed more deeply as everyone laughed at him. Bill knew the kid well enough by now to understand Josh's aversion to "secondhand" women—the kid's prim phrase for sexually forward women. However, that angelic face and quality clothing of hers had won the little prig over.

"Do you follow a profession, Miss Jackson?" the reporter inquired.

"When I must," she replied with charming candor. "I've done many things since I left Boston. Been a faro dealer in New Orleans, taught school in St. Louis, and I've written travel sketches for the ladies' press back east."

"I'm with the press, too," Josh tossed in eagerly. "The *New York Herald*."

"Ain't it *all* the ladies' press?" Bill asked from a deadpan. Josh flushed again, and Bill just shook his head.

Hickok made a deliberate point of keeping his distance from Sandra Jackson—or whoever she really was. He was intensely aware that one other person was watching them from the rear of the grazing herd. The last thing he needed right now was to ignite a jealous Calamity Jane's fuse.

"All right, men!" Matt called out. "This isn't Fiddler's Green, it's the Chisholm Trail! Let's push some beef north!"

"They say a deserter never sleeps," Olney Lucas told his brother. "Well, the mighty Bill goddamn Hickok better stay wide awake, too."

The Lucas boys crouched on a sandy slope just east of the cattle trail. Olney had selected this spot as perfect for exploiting a deadly combination: Jip's dark talent at the killing arts, and Olney's keen brain for harnessing that talent.

"Just a little bit more," Jip said, watching his brother pour black powder into a small hole. "A little more . . . little more . . . nuff!"

Both men knelt behind a huge boulder that sat on the top of the slope. The slope was steep, perhaps sixty degrees or sharper, but scalable. It was littered with loose talus and scree, deposited eons earlier by glacial movement.

Olney, who had read up on mine engineering

when he was in prison, knew all about "angle of repose"—the critical point at which an object succumbs to the pull of gravity. This big rock was on the verge of that critical angle. The moment the black-powder charge exploded, the boulder would go smashing downward. And much of the unstable slope would go with it.

Of course, a man would need to be lured up here close, where escape would be impossible. And that's where Olney's sick genius factored into the equation. He glanced again at a narrow ledge just below them, a thin outcropping of metamorphic rock.

A friendly-looking, but clearly distressed, hound dog whined repeatedly up at them as if asking why they had tossed him down into this spot. The dog could not get enough traction to climb upward to them. And the jump off the ledge, to the trail below, was at least fifty feet.

Olney had used raw antelope meat to lure the friendly mutt away from a farm just east of the Chisholm Trail. Anyone who had read about James Butler Hickok knew that he liked dogs as much as he liked horses. During his early days as a stagecoach and freight driver, out in the old Spanish land-grant country of New Mexico, Hickok often had a canine companion for company and security—most domesticated dogs reacted loudly to the Indian smell.

"This is perfect," Olney said again. "What's to suspect? Hickok rides by alone, out scouting. The dog sees him, cries for help. Hickok looks up, and what's he see? Why, just some poor mutt that must've took a tumble while chasing squirrels."

Jip ignored his younger brother, fingers deftly attaching a fuse of bright orange detonating cord.

"Each foot of fuse burns thirty seconds," he informed Olney. "How long you want it?"

"Short. Short as you can make it and still leave us time to clear the blast after we light it. Hickok might hear it, and we don't want to give him time to react."

Jip nodded and crimped the cord at about three inches, maybe six or seven seconds. Olney watched, marveling. He had no idea why or how Jip had developed such talent with explosive charges. He was a soft-brain, kicked in the head by a mule when he was only two years old.

What was it that doc in Montana called him? A whatchacallit, an idiot-savant. Stupid and slow in most things, but, in his case, with a genius for killing.

This same kind of explosive charge had worked brilliantly up in Wyoming's South Pass country. They had literally blown a stagecoach into a canyon far below, then simply picked out the valuables of the dead like vultures plucking out eyeballs.

"Done," Jip announced, standing up and wiping his hands on his filthy buckskin trousers.

Something occurred to Olney. "Hell's bells! Good chance the blast'll ruin Hickok's face."

He looked at his brother. "Got your skinnin' knife?"

Jip nodded. "In my saddle pocket."

"Good man. We'll lift his dander. Them gold curls, plus his guns, will prove the deed."

The dog below them howled in dismay when the two men continued to ignore him.

"Hang tough, pooch," Olney called down to it. "Your savior is a-comin'!"

Wild Bill turned Fire-away over to Mosley, their harried but capable wrangler, and selected a fresh mount for the day's second stint of scouting duty.

"Anybody rode that bay yet today?" Bill asked, nodding toward one of the horses with the four-sixes brand on its hip.

"He's fresh as new bread," Johnny Reb assured him. "Good hoss, too. I looked in his mouth—he ain't even six years old yet."

"Dolph Reynolds called him 'a reg'lar sort of cow pony,' " Bill told the private. "In Texas, that means better than any horse in Illinois."

Bill transferred his rigging from Fire-way to the new mount, all the time keeping a speculative eye on Sandra Jackson. She had climbed onto the board seat of the buckboard, chatting animatedly to Rob Meadows.

Mosley saw Bill watching her, and the lad grinned. "She's truly a little peach, Wild Bill. I sure-God envy you."

"A peach," Bill reminded him, "is soft outside, but like a stone inside."

"Just enjoy the outside part," Mosley drawled, and both men laughed.

Bill stepped up and over, kicking both feet into the stirrups. "Just remember, Reb, she ain't carrying my brand or any other that I can see. Any man on this drive can try his luck with her—cards or otherwise. Just don't forget: Even the devil can cite Scripture for his purposes."

Reb, who had seen something of the larger world before he enlisted, now confided: "Since you bring that up, Wild Bill, I figure her for a grifter."

Bill nodded. "But then, I've never known a beautiful woman who wasn't, one way or another."

Reb grinned and nodded back. "She'll liven up the trip. I'm glad you fetched her back."

Hickok wheeled his mount and rode out of camp. He mulled the woman's story as he loped the bay out across the rolling land dotted with juniper and stunted little scrub oaks. The cactus had thinned out rapidly as the trail wound north toward the next river, the Brazos.

Bill didn't believe her story. But people lied for a host of reasons. His problem was in deciding her motivation. He suspected she was simply a wily opportunist who exploited men in a woman-starved country.

If she was a grifter, a con artist, fine. If her sole intent was to fleece the gullible men out of their cash, one way or another, then let them live and learn. Bill wasn't religious, but he believed in God. And he also believed God made some women smart and beautiful to offset some of the male bullies with muscles.

119

There was always the chance, however, that she was part of something more sinister and deadly—a plot to kill him and scuttle this drive.

Even as all this looped through his mind, Hickok kept his eyes in steady motion. The rolling scrubland was showing more variety now, including rock formations and stretches where it was sliced by deep gullies washed red with eroded soil.

Wind-whipped grit slapped his face, and Bill pulled down his hat against the swirling dust. Soon he became aware of a dog barking—the monotonous yelping of a dog feeling desolate and doomed.

The sandy ground, on both sides of the wide wash that served as trail, rose in steep banks. Bill glanced high up on the right and spotted it: a dog marooned on a little rock shelf.

The dog flew into a pleading frenzy upon spotting him. Bill reined in the bay, gazing thoughtfully upward.

By long habit, he considered if this was a trap. He couldn't rule it out. But Bill knew dogs well, especially hounds like this one. They often followed their keen noses into trouble just like this. Bill had pulled stuck dogs out of hollow logs, too, and once he had rescued one from an ice floe on the Snake River.

"Slow and easy, boy," Wild Bill coaxed his mount as they started up the slope. The bay didn't like this, but was too loyal to rebel. Even days from now, Bill would still be remembering this moment with acute guilt.

He eased his Winchester out of its boot, butt plate resting on his right thigh. Seeing the man riding up, the dog stopped barking and switched to welcoming whimpers. Bill kept his '72 ready, but his first, deepest suspicion had passed.

"Steady, boy," he soothed the bay. The unfamiliar dog made the horse prick its ears. But it continued to climb the slope, carefully searching for traction in the sand.

A minute later, Bill whistled once and the grateful mutt leaped into his lap, almost knocking Bill from the saddle. Bill turned his face away in disgust from the mutt's lapping tongue.

Just then the bay flinched, snuffing the ground cautiously. It's got a whiff of man scent, Bill assumed with reflexive quickness, and in that same instant the Winchester repeater was tucked under his arm, ready for a target.

In the expectant stillness, he heard a sickeningly familiar hissing and sputtering noise, coming from above, behind that big rock.

Fear hammered at his temples, but Bill didn't let his fright cost him a moment of reaction time.

His war days had already taught him that most men survive a close blast by lunging at a right angle to the forward thrust. Savagely, Wild Bill gouged his spurs into the bay's tender shoulders, and it reacted as any spirited horse would: It deliberately leaped high and jackknifed, tossing Bill, the dog still in his grip, off to the right even as the slope exploded in a murderous cascade of rocks and scree.

The main blast thrust was so close that debris tore the heel off Wild Bill's left boot, while the noise left both ears ringing. The bay was killed instantly. But that last-second leap had tossed Bill and the dog just beyond the deadly blast pattern.

Unfortunately, Hickok's legendary luck ran out when he landed; unable to break his fall, he saw starbursts inside his skull when the back of his neck slammed into a rock. Bill didn't lose consciousness, but the fall had momentarily stunned major nerves in his spine.

The frightened but uninjured hound tore off down the slope, but loyally returned when it realized Bill hadn't moved. Even as it frantically licked the man's face, urging him to move, Wild Bill Hickok got the worst fright of his eventful life.

As he lay immobile on the slope, unable to move from the neck down, two men suddenly emerged from the clearing smoke, bearing down on Hickok at a run, howling in triumph like madmen.

One—the smallest, a cocky little banty rooster— threw a rifle into his shoulder socket and, halting, began taking up the trigger slack. And the other one, Bill realized with numb shock, carried a curved skinning knife!

Chapter Ten

Had Wild Bill been an Indian, he would have sung his death song right then. He could twitch his left foot, but that was it. Even as the cocky little bastard with the bolt-action Berdan took up the trigger slack, Bill's stunned nerve pinned him helpless as a bug under a needle.

"Well, *shit*," he said, his voice only mildly irritated as he drew what augured to be his last breath.

A gun detonated, and Bill twitched in anticipation of death. Instead, blood blossomed from the rifleman's left thigh, and he howled in pain.

"You sawed-off, bushwhackin' peckerwood!" Calamity Jane's voice brayed from below on the trail. "If you've kilt Bill Hickok, I'll slice you open from neck to nuts!"

Her huge, hog-leg pistol tossed more lead upward, but it was a tricky angle even for a crack shot like Jane. The dullard-looking man with the curved knife proved a very loyal companion, Hickok noted—even as Jane kept the air lively around them, he tossed the wounded man over his shoulder and fled down the back slope.

"Jesus, Jane, cease fire!" Bill beseeched her. "You'll kill me with ricochets, girl!"

"Goldang it, if you can yell," Jane grumped as she urged Ignatius up the slope, "hie after them sorry sons of bitches, Bill. Or did they plug you?"

"Got stunned in the explosion," Bill explained. "Aww, Christ!" he added when he saw the bloody remains of the bay.

"I heard the boom. Sure tossed some landscape around," Jane marveled. "Whoa there, Ignatius!"

The well-trained camel, though clearly upset by the pungent odor of spent cordite and blood, held steady as Jane climbed down and knelt close to Bill.

"Lady," he greeted her in a grateful tone, "you could sure use a bath. But I'm glad to see you."

"Hell, a bunch of clerks take baths," Jane scoffed.

"This makes twice now you've covered my six on this cattle drive."

"Un-hunh. And there you lay," Jane said speculatively, "all helpless and purdy."

Her eyes dropped to his belt. The sudden gleam in her bloodshot, jaundiced eyeballs made Bill's face break out in sweat.

"Now, hold on there, I'm stunned," he reminded her. "Can't function."

"Bet I can make *one* part of you set up and take notice."

Bill could move both feet now as more and more feeling returned to his lower body. Dear Lord, at least give me a chance to run. . . .

"Hallo!" shouted Matt's voice from below, and Wild Bill gave silent thanks.

"Aww, *hell*," Jane carped.

"Up here, Matt!" Bill sang out.

Soon the debris-littered slope was crowded as first Matt, then Joshua and Abel Langford, clambered up.

Bill could sit up by now and rub his sore neck.

"Get a look at 'em, Wild Bill?" Matt asked. The young officer had already checked the back slope, but the attackers were well out across the flats, making good time on strong horses.

Bill nodded. "I think one of 'em was the same jasper tried to air me out back at the river."

Joshua had remained silent, stricken with guilt. Now he spoke up. "You think it was my story set them on you?"

Bill shrugged an indifferent shoulder. "What's after what's next?"

Josh frowned. "Hunh?"

"That's what I say, too," Bill retorted. "Hunh? How'm I spozed to know if they're just freelance profiteers or sent down by Harding Ott? A bullet's a bullet when you're the target."

By the time Bill was on his feet again, the late-afternoon light had taken on that mellow richness just before sunset. He caught a ride back to camp on the rear of Matt's big sorrel.

As it turned out, that confrontation had evidently taken some of the steam out of Wild Bill's stalkers. The next week or so along the trail was blessedly free of deadly attacks.

They caught another big break: This late in summer the rivers were lower and slower. They forded the Brazos with impunity, simply driving the buckboard over on a gravel spit.

Wild Bill, his conscience stinging him, invited Calamity Jane to come up into the camp circle with the rest at night. But she stoutly refused—that near miss on the slope had almost cost her the love of her young life. Keeping Hickok alive, she believed with religious fervor, was her mission in life. She started staying out beyond camp at night, a sort of roving vedette.

The drive made good time, but all was not beer and skittles. Selecting a bed ground each night became trickier, for much of the ground now was covered with worthless cheatgrass.

The herd, too, was getting salty. Now and then, for reasons of their own, the cattle simply took a notion to scatter hither and yon. The swing men were hard-pressed, at times, to keep the longhorns bunched.

With all his other pressing duties, Wild Bill also found time to flirt with Sandra Jackson. He was beginning to believe she was merely a sly con artist, not a hired assassin.

For one thing, she had already cleaned out all the men at poker. And naturally she had challenged "the luckiest man in the world" to play, winning his entire $60 stake in two nights. Bill knew she cheated, somehow crimping or marking the cards. But he couldn't catch her, and that impressed him.

Only three days after crossing the Brazos, they forded the Trinity River just west of Forth Worth.

"Okay if I ride into town and file my dispatch?" Josh asked Bill. "There's a Western Union there."

"What about the drag slot? We can't hold up the drive just so you can file your lies."

"Jane offered to ride it—on a horse."

"Then go ahead," Bill told the kid, slipping him three silver dollars. "Pick me up a bottle of Old Taylor and some stogies. Bring back a newspaper, too."

"What are you two handsome devils plotting?" Sandra challenged them, emerging from her tent and still brushing out her beautiful mane of chestnut hair.

"Longfellow here is riding into Forth Worth," Bill informed her. "This is your big chance."

Those striking, nutshell-shaped eyes looked at Bill curiously. "My big chance to what?"

"Why, to arrange for faster, more comfortable accommodations to Wichita," Bill said. "There's a Midland Stage office there."

"More comfortable and faster, perhaps," she replied. "But safer? You forget I tried the stage from Louisiana with disastrous results. This way I've got a dozen soldiers to protect me—not to mention the luckiest man in the world," she added, blowing him a little kiss.

Bill watched her close as he said, "Aren't you worried about that ailing mother of yours hanging on until you get there?"

She didn't miss a beat. "Oh, pouf. Mother's always been melodramatic. It's probably just her lumbago acting up."

All that was fine, Bill thought cynically, except for one little detail. In her original story it was her father who was ailing. Don't get too careless around that one, Bill resolved again. He still remembered her reply, a few nights ago, when Joshua asked her if she had a philosophy of life.

"But of course," she had replied, flashing that restive smile as she scooped in her winnings. "A gal must have a backbone, not a wishbone."

Joshua caught up with the cattle drive later that afternoon, so mad he was muttering to himself.

"Here's your damned newspaper," he fumed, handing Bill that day's issue of the *Fort Worth Messenger.* "Look. Tom Van Dyke, my number-one rival back east, has trumped me with a damned pack of lies!"

Wild Bill glanced at the headline on page one:

HICKOK'S MISFITS DEFEAT
RUSTLING GANG IN
CATTLE-TRAIL SHOOT-OUT!

It was an Associated Press release. Hickok laughed outright at the clearly fabricated account. Van Dyke cleverly avoided any legal charges later with such phrases as "according to an eyewitness" and "sources close to the scene."

"Hell, says here I shot three and killed two more with a bowie knife," Hickok bragged. "This is damn fine writing. Pure poetry."

"It's pure dreck! Just hack fiction!"

"Best kind, Junior. Pays the bills, no pun."

Secretly, Wild Bill welcomed the foolish pack of lies. It reinforced the illusion of his "charmed life," thus discouraging attacks. Also, being all lies, it failed to pinpoint his location.

"Shuck on back to the drag slot," Hickok added when Josh continued fretting and moping. "You're a cowboy now, not a scribbler."

That night, after a swift but brilliant copper sunset, Calamity Jane set out on her night-riding rounds. Sandra and a few of the men with a penny left to their name were playing poker near the campfire. A biscuit pan propped up on rocks was their table.

Wild Bill usually joined the game after supper. Tonight, though, he took his bottle of Old Taylor and walked out to a low hill with a good view of the surrounding area. Moonlight was generous— he wanted to drink in peace and reconnoiter a bit.

His stomach, once cast iron, was finally starting to rebel after years of frontier abuse. Bill was forced to water his liquor tonight, and he felt long in the tooth. A man who couldn't drink his liquor neat didn't belong on the trail, he reminded himself as he poured water into his canteen cup.

A twig snapped behind him, and Bill instantly tucked and rolled, coming up with a .44 in his right fist.

"My soul alive!" Sandra greeted him in the ghostly moonlight, gaping at the blued steel.

"Lady, you're *lucky* it's still alive," he assured her, holstering his Peacemaker. "It ain't a good idea to sneak up on a fellow after dark."

She watched him pick his cup back up and wipe it off on his sleeve.

"I didn't 'sneak,' " she pouted. "I saw your bottle earlier. I merely came out to see if a girl can get a drink around here."

Bill whiffed her gardenia perfume. She wore a full skirt that emphasized her small, tight waist.

"I can offer you bourbon and ditch water," he joked, handing her his cup.

"May I ask you something?" she said after taking down the contents by two inches. "I confess my vanity is wounded. To be perfectly blunt about it, Mr. Hickok, I have given you several opportunities to . . . ahhmm, shall I say, to enjoy a pas de deux with me? You have declined each time."

She stepped even closer, and Bill felt the animal warmth radiating from her. Steady, old son, he cautioned himself. This gal could follow you into a revolving door and come out ahead.

"In fact," she continued, "I've come to the conclusion that Wild Bill Hickok is sufficiently interested in me to be cruel, but no more."

"That dog don't hunt," he assured her. "I'm plenty interested."

"Then what is it? What, a woman who makes the first move is a whore? Is that it?"

Bill studied her with mild humor in his eyes. "I got no problem with a literal whore. I respect the work ethic. But then there's the other kind of whoring—making a whore of your soul."

"What's got into you?" she challenged. "Religion?"

"No. Just the desire to keep on living."

One of Bill's hands dipped into the big front pocket of his canvas duster. He produced her little alligator jewel case.

"This little hideout gun of yours could rip a man's face off. Or are you a back-shooter?"

For just a moment she lost her confident composure. Then she went on the offensive. Even in moonlight, Bill saw red splotches of anger leap into her cheeks. "You went through my valise!"

"Guilty as charged. It's my cattle drive."

She turned away from him with the grace of a ballerina standing on her pointes. But instead of storming away, she turned back around to confront him.

"Mr. Hickok, do *you* travel unarmed in the American West?"

"That might prove bad for my longevity," he quipped. "But that's me. Plenty of men don't carry weapons out here, Sandra. However, that's not my point. You're a gambler, a hideout gun comes with the territory."

She looked confused. "Then why this accusation?"

"You were supposedly abducted, remember? Those thieves let you keep your piece, huh?"

"I . . . that is, they . . ." She gave up, flashing Hickok a woebegone smile.

"Oh, all right, I lied," she confessed. "My name isn't Sandra Jackson, either. It's Felicity Parker. Fel. I'm a con, pure and simple. There was no robbery. I read in the papers about you and this cattle drive. I confess—I just mainly wanted to . . . meet you."

Fel knew she was gambling here by telling some of the truth. She had decided one *can* have her cake and eat it, too. Of course, she still meant to collect that $25,000 for killing Hickok. But why make haste when she could have a little fun first?

For his part, Wild Bill could find no hole in this latest story. It reminded him that the snooty class back east complained incessantly that life out west was boring and monotonous. But as this woman proved all over again, there were too many radically different types on the frontier for life to ever be boring for long.

He handed the little jewel case back to her. "I'm flattered by the trouble you took to . . . meet me," he told her.

"Shouldn't you search me?" she suggested. "Make sure I don't have any more weapons hidden?"

She wasn't being sarcastic, so Bill took her up on the offer.

"There's plenty here," he reported a minute later. "But nothing hard or dangerous."

"Hard and dangerous," she replied, her voice husky, "is *your* job. The man is the gun, the woman is the holster—don't you know that?"

"Like they say in Missouri," Bill told her, lowering his mouth to hers, "show me."

Chapter Eleven

Harding Ott was not the type who panicked. Still, he *was* starting to worry.

He had not expected any progress reports from Fel; she wasn't free to send telegrams or dispatch the new express messengers offered by the Midland Stagecoach Line. However, the word from the Lucas brothers did not sound promising. Hickok still walked the earth, the cattle drive was in full swing, and Olney was laid up with a gunshot wound.

Ott was still hopeful that Fel would come through once she had herself a little fun with Hickok. She was a creature of strange passions, and it was just like her to thrill at seducing a man before she killed him.

But the town-site developer never counted on any plan without a backup. Or, as he put it: Every country wind has its city cousin. So he called a meeting of his top Indian lackeys, Bobcat and Chinook.

"I'm not saying there *will* be a set-to up here," he assured them. "I don't think it'll come to that. I'm just saying we need to be ready."

Bobcat translated a few words to help Chinook, whose English was weak. By now Ott regretted telling Woman Dress to serve coffee instead of whiskey. When sober, these two braves remembered they were Lakotas, not white men's dogs.

"Woman Dress," Ott called to his Crow slave. "I almost forgot—bring us the gifts I have selected for our guests."

Woman Dress immediately rose from the cowhide stool where she always sat, attending her owner's wishes but staying out of the way. She cast her eyes down in shame as the two visitors—sober now and thus harsher toward her—cast scornful glances at her.

They could see how her slim belly was now swelling with Ott's child. Ott had always preferred Indian concubines because they weren't headstrong like white women. He had fathered "bastards born with sunburns" all over the West, from the Marias to the Rio Grande. He had abandoned every child to live a despised life in a no-man's-land, rejected by both races.

Woman Dress ducked behind a ratty old horse blanket that served as a bedroom door. When she returned, her two visitors stared at the handsome revolvers in hand-tooled leather holsters.

"For you, my red friends," Ott said, using the

ceremonial formality that always impressed Indians. "Brand-new single-action .44s. That lever on the right side of the frame extracts the cartridge. Fires as fast as you can cock it."

He showed them how to work the mechanism. All of the Indian policemen already had good rifles. But no Sioux on the reservation owned a side arm of any kind—symbols of white man's power. Ott knew exactly how to dupe red men—lure them with all the trappings of manhood, denied to them by treaty.

Both visitors admired the weapons as Ott went on.

"Like I said, I don't think it'll come to a battle up here. But if it does, we must be ready. I'm riding out later to get the lay of the land where they'll be crossing the South Platte."

When Bobcat finished translating for his friend, Ott said: "Also tell him this, Bobcat. Each policeman who fights like a Lakota will receive a fine pony for his string and a case of whiskey. Not Indian burner, either. I mean fine white man's whiskey."

Carefully, Jip Lucas pried the slug off a brass shell casing. Olney watched him tamp the load tight with the head of a spike, then pack the shell with extra grains of powder.

"That's the gait," Olney approved. "The bullet's accuracy won't matter. We just need the noise."

The Lucas boys had fled north into the vast Indian Territory, the federal set-aside north of the

Red River that had become an outlaw haven. They holed up in an abandoned mud-and-lumber dugout so Olney's wound could knit.

"Never mind Bill goddamn Hickok," Olney said. "It's the *herd* them Injuns will eat. So we'll scatter 'em. And we'll kill soldiers until they ain't got the manpower to bunch and hold them cows."

Jip used crimping pliers to reattach the slug to the powder charge. Olney thumbed it through the breech of his Berdan and jacked it into the chamber.

"After today," Olney added, "they'll be across the Red. The herd'll be all nerved up from the ford. We'll stampede 'em tonight during the dog watch. Hickok ain't got no idea in hell just how far it is to Nebraska when the Lucas brothers are dogging you."

Hickok's Misfits found favor with Lady Luck, and they had smooth sailing into the vast Indian Territory. The only incident of note occurred at Red River Station. A submerged log spooked Joshua's coyote dun in midstream, and it bucked the reporter into the river.

Josh couldn't swim, and for a moment he was in real danger of drowning. But Wild Bill had yelled out to him, "Grab a steer's tail, Longfellow!" It worked beautifully, and Joshua was towed safely to shallower water.

Only Hickok had the experience to truly appreciate this effortless, fast crossing. He was glad it was late in the season, and the water down. Back in '71, some thirty outfits with more than sixty thousand cattle were trapped there waiting for flood waters to subside. Cows were backed up for forty miles, and grass became damn scarce.

At midday, Bill called a halt to graze the herd, as he always did. The men all stripped their sweat-drenched saddle blankets, drying them in the baking sun.

At Matt's tireless urging, each man also carefully inspected his mount. Gall salve was applied when needed, and the horses' hooves were inspected for cracks or loose shoes.

"Been pretty quiet past few days," Josh remarked as he, Bill, and Matt paused for hot coffee and biscuits left over from breakfast—standard fare at midday, just to tide them until supper.

"What you really mean," Bill said, "is that nobody's tried to plant me."

"That trap with the dog," Josh reminded him, "was the third try. You said once that for you trouble comes in threes. Maybe that's the end of it."

Wild Bill sweetened the bitter coffee with a lump of *piloncillo,* a crude brown sugar favored by Mexicans.

"Sure," he told the kid tonelessly. "And the world has grown honest since we rode out of San Antone."

A woman's voice could be heard singing "Little Brown Jug"—Fel Parker, still Sandra Jackson to everyone but Bill, was busy at a nearby creek, washing out some frilly underclothes.

"She's sure been in a good mood lately," Josh hinted. "And so have you."

"Hell, I'm always sweet," Bill assured him. He was squatting by his gear, holding a small mirror as he carefully combed out his mustache.

If the rest of the men had noticed that Bill and their pretty passenger tended to take walks frequently, after dark, no one was saying anything—openly.

But Bill knew Joshua was miffed. Their pretty passenger seemed completely unimpressed by his newspaper credentials. The kid didn't understand how a gal could ignore a man who read Plato and spoke French, sort of. Man alive, Josh had written to his mother, the culture out here was coarse!

Matt cast a bleak glance around at the barren landscape. "The government didn't cede this land to Indians because it's lush. How's water up ahead, Bill?"

"Nothing but alkali sinks before the Washita. After that we'll be fine until we're north of the Cimarron. But what worries me most, for the next week or so, is stampedes. This is flat, open ground with damned little to impede a full-bore run."

"I better put a third man on herd guard, huh?"

Bill nodded. "Keep Otis riding as long as he can stay awake. That man's singing could calm a sore-tailed bear."

"I'll talk at the men tonight," Matt decided. "Reinforce the nighttime silence rule."

Again Bill agreed with a nod. Just yesterday a sharp-tailed grouse had whirred up while the herd was grazing, startling a lead bull. If Abel Langford had not reacted as quickly as he did, cutting at sharp angles to block the bull from running, they might have lost the herd or much of it.

Calamity Jane rode back in as Bill was riding out for the day's second stint of scouting. By now Fire-away accepted Ignatius—at a wary distance. Steeling himself, Bill saluted his self-appointed guardian angel.

"See any trouble out there, Jane?"

"If I see it, I'll shoot it," she vowed. She cocked a sour eye at him. Bill was downwind, but couldn't sort out the camel stink from the Jane stink.

"Do me a favor, Bill?"

"Hell, I sure owe you a few."

"Next time you diddle that fine-boned missy of yours, *don't* do it ten feet from my bedroll!"

The unflappable Bill Hickok actually blushed. Jane barked in contempt.

"And you talk about Joshua coloring up like a girl," Jane teased him.

"I didn't know we were intruding on you, Jane," Wild Bill muttered. "Gets dark outside the camp circle."

"Why, good God a-gorry! You two're like dogs in heat! If I hadn't been stone-dead drunk, I'd've poured cold water on you both."

"When you shadow a man, Jane," he reproached her mildly, "you can't blame him for what you don't need to see."

"Why, you vain jackass! If I *didn't* dog your tail, you'd be feeding worms by now."

"Can't gainsay that," Bill admitted, not liking the fact much. He touched his hat and rode out.

"Bill?"

He looked over his shoulder. "Yeah?"

"Watch your topknot. It's too quiet out there. Graveyard quiet, if you take my drift."

Despite Jane's dire warning, good luck held. Bill returned in late afternoon and halted the drive on a reasonably good patch of graze. There was no water for the herd, but they had tanked up good the day before and were holding up. The horses were given small amounts of water from a gutbag tied to the chuck wagon, rationed by Meadows.

Despite Felicity's proximity and plentiful charms, Wild Bill rolled into his blankets early tonight. Too much scouting, too many dalliances, and advancing age were taking their combined toll. The camp noises, subdued by the silence rule, were a pleasant mutter in his ears as he rapidly fell into a deep and dreamless sleep, his favorite kind.

The quiet, here in the desolate, scrubland vastness of the Indian Territory, was as perfect and complete as that of a crypt. But sometime during the last hours before dawn, all hell erupted, beginning with a shattering boom like a small cannon.

Bill rolled out of his blankets and kicked up the fire even before he came fully awake. In those first confused moments, the war was on again. The gathering rumble of stampeding cattle was the Southern Cavalry charging.

Before his mind could clear away the sleep cobwebs, he shouted: "They've breached our pickets! Up and on the line!"

Moments later he woke up in the present. Matt, across the way, was also sitting up, and already the camp was boiling with rushing men.

"Stampede!" Bill roared out. "Mosley, protect the remuda! Swing men, drag rider, everybody—all of us haze the cows clockwise, throw 'em into a mill!"

Bill, not even bothering with his boots, cut Fireaway out of the nervous, sidestepping horses and vaulted on him. Not only was he riding bareback, he had to count on the gelding's instincts to guide them without the control of bit and reins.

One thing Bill's early days as a Pony Express rider had taught him was how to hang on under rough conditions. He hunkered low and far forward, like a jockey, grabbing fistfuls of mane to hold on. The ground rumbled from fleeing cattle, and already a choking cloud of dust obscured the moon in haze.

The men had been told what to do in a stampede, but this was their first test. The horses, at least, knew what to do, although the Cavalry mounts were far less agile than Dolph's ponies. Still, they showed good bottom in overtaking and crowding the herd.

Wild Bill watched a bull start to break back to the south, taking other animals with him. Bill boldly cut off the bull's escape and turned him north. But it almost cost his horse a goring when the bull lunged at Fire-away, missing by scant inches.

At some point in the confusion, gunshots erupted from amid the bawling, thunderous melee. Hickok cursed. He had ordered the men *never* to use gunshots for herding. But it was easy to lose your head in a full-bore run like this.

The mad charge seemed to go on forever. But slowly, steadily, like a cyclone finally blowing itself out, their efforts began to check the stampede. From its widely scattered pattern, the herd was gradually bunched, then funneled in on itself, running in a harmless circle until they finally halted, exhausted.

Now, Bill fretted, they'll want water.

He spotted Matt's officer's hat. "Better account for your men," Bill told him. "Then set herd guards out."

Matt seemed not to hear him. Now Bill glimpsed the hard set of his jaw. "What is it, son?"

"I just counted heads," Matt replied in a stricken tone. "Otis Jones is dead, Wild Bill."

Hickok felt a cold sickness low in his guts. "Trampled?"

Matt shook his head. Even in moonlight, Bill saw the muscles bunch tight where Matt's jaw hinged. "Shot, Bill. Twice in the back."

Hickok recalled those gunshots he had attributed to careless soldiers. But of course, it was the same shooter who had spooked the herd. Now the cold sickness passed, replaced by a white-hot, burning anger.

"That's it, then," he told Matt. "I figured we only had trouble with money grubbers out to sell my plew. But stampeding the herd and killing Otis—these are Harding Ott's dirt workers. They mean to make sure this herd doesn't get through."

"Well, they *will* get through," Matt swore. "Come hell or high water."

"We've had the high water," Bill assured him. "Now get set for the hell part."

Chapter Twelve

Lieutenant Matt Carlson was no preacher. But he spoke the eulogy at Otis Jones's funeral, and his voice carried with conviction in that quiet prairie vastness.

"Most of you men don't know it because Otis was a modest man. But he was a hero during the Great Rebellion. The Rebs made a charge on Vicksburg. Otis grabbed the flag and rallied untrained Negro recruits in a skirmish against battle-hardened Rebels. They stopped the Confederate States Army dead in their tracks at a spot called Milliken's Bend. Otis was shot three times, but he refused to fall and let Mr. Lincoln's flag touch the ground."

"Well, God kiss me," Hickok spoke up with deep surprise and respect. "So Otis was the fellow we

145

all called 'Cannon Ball' Jones! He saved at least one thousand Billy Yanks that day."

After Bill's first flush of surprise and respect, however, the white-hot anger returned. To think that two murdering, back-shooting prairie rats took down such a soldier's soldier—but he tried to think more peacefully as Otis's lonely grave was slowly filled.

By Cavalry tradition, each man took a turn at the shovel, Bill and Matt included. An empty shell casing had been nailed to the crude wooden cross. Inside, also by tradition, was a small piece of rolled-up paper. It contained the names of every man in the detail.

Despite her earlier anger and jealousy at Felicity, the sentimental Calamity Jane joined her, arm in arm, when Fel started openly sobbing.

Later, when Joshua's account of this sad occasion appeared nationally, even Wild Bill would praise the lad's simple but fitting tribute:

There was no bugler to play "Taps." But the assembled soldiers sang two songs to honor their fallen hero: the sad dirge "I Once Had A Comrade," and the religious hymn "Rock of Ages." More than one strong man thumbed a tear from his eyes as this noble soldier was sent to report for his last duty station in Paradise.

A solemn Matt did not exhort the men to vengeance. But as the ceremony ended and the men went back to work, he remarked quietly, "Just remember, men. We're the Cavalry, and the Cavalry never forgets."

"Yes, SIR!" the men popped off as one. Bill knew what the men secretly felt, because he shared in it: blood lust. An incredible amount of crime was tolerated out west, even including some petty rustling. But horse thieves, barn burners, and back-shooters were hounded into hell itself.

Unfortunately, Wild Bill had a more pressing problem as he rode out in the vanguard—finding water for the herd.

"Those beeves sweat hard when they run," he explained to Matt. "That fandango last night evaporated two, three days' worth of water from them."

Matt nodded, his young face troubled. "And you were already worried how this is the driest stretch," Matt fretted. "What now?"

"No relief, according to the map, until the Washita. I'll try to find water before. Meantime, tell the men it's important to keep a close eye on the herd. The thirstier they get, the more the danger they'll sull on us. Out here, that means they stop and die. It ain't pretty."

But though he tried every survival trick he knew, Wild Bill could not scout out any worthwhile amount of water. He watched where the birds flew in the morning; he dug into dry streambeds; he even gave Fire-away free rein for hours, hoping the roan would nose out some water. But nothing worked.

"Dry as a year-old cow chip," he reported to Matt at noon on the day after they buried Otis. "I did at least find a lot of sotol stalks. I marked the locations. Send men out to chop up the roots. They hold a little moisture—we can feed it to the beeves at night."

Even as he spoke, Bill noticed Felicity near the chuck wagon. She appeared lost in thought, idly cooling her face with a graceful little fan of white net with gold sequins. To Bill, she'd seemed moody and subdued since Otis had been killed.

Nothing very strange there, Wild Bill admitted. After all, these men had adopted her, and she them. But her preoccupation seemed to go a little deeper than mere sympathy.

"Lady, you look like somebody kicked your dog," he greeted her. "Still thinking about Otis?"

She nodded, giving him a rueful smile.

"Soldiers die," Bill reminded her. "It's hard duty out here. If a bullet doesn't tag you, dysentery or a rattlesnake will."

"I know," she conceded. "And I've seen plenty of death. It's just . . . back east they take a lot for granted. When they're hungry, western beef will be in the shops, fresh and cheap. But their easy life back there is paid for out here in blood and toil."

Right as rain, thought Bill. And paid for by lonely, underpaid, underfed, overworked men who aren't welcome in the "fine society" they feed and protect. Cowboys, soldiers, teamsters, stock tenders, blacksmiths, railroad workers, miners . . . the men, in short, who built America out of raw wilderness.

He took in the pearly allure of her skin. Bill thought about that muff gun he'd returned to her. Despite being his lover now, she might still have plans to use it. He had no illusions, and that's why he was still alive.

Well, the gun was hers, wasn't it? Bill's code regarding firearms was fair and simple: Only proven criminals were to be disarmed.

Hickok rode out ahead again that afternoon, searching hard for water. The drive was still days from the Washita, with no moisture for the cattle except sotol roots.

Wild Bill had been following a long, low ridge for some time, searching for signs of an underground aquifer rumored to be in this area. Abruptly, gunshots—too distant to immediately alarm him—erupted from the opposite side of the ridge.

Soon a pitched gun battle was in progress. Bill swung down and low-crawled up the ridge to the crest for a better view.

The moment he saw the scenario below, Bill loosed a whistle.

"So our dry-gulchers are at it again. Jane, *how* did you ride into a trap like that?"

Ignatius lay sprawled on the ground in a sandy wash, and the awkward position of his legs told Bill he'd been shot out from under Jane. Now she was using her dead mount as a breastworks, firing back at her attackers.

Bill could see very quickly, however, that she could not get a decent bead on them. He spotted the bulwark of stones they had built on a low hill. They had a clear line of fire from high ground.

And one of them, Bill had to admit, was a crackerjack shot. It was the little, cocky one with the fancy bolt-action rifle. Again and again he fired, sending little dust puffs rising from the dead camel every time a round struck.

Far from being scared, Calamity Jane was still enraged at the death of her beloved camel.

"You milk-kneed, white-livered, needle-dick bug-humpers!" she roared out. "Real *men*, ain'tchers, shooting an unarmed camel!"

"Yeah, and you're next, you ugly hell hag!" the banty rooster shouted back. "Nobody shoots Olney Lucas and walks away from it."

Hearing the name, Bill knew instantly who these two hardtails were: Jip and Olney Lucas, known up in the northwest country as the Black Rock Boys after their home range in the Nevada desert. Killers, thieves, train robbers, even a bank vault expertly blown open in Carson City had been attributed to them.

Bill glanced all around, throwing together a plan. He left Fire-away hobbled below the ridge, safe. Hickok had already lost one good horse to these bastards—he refused to make a target of Fire-away on this wide-open prairie.

He did, however, return to his horse. Bill opened a saddle pocket and removed a handy little invention he had taken from Frank Tutt, a resourceful hardcase he killed last year in New Mexico Territory. It was a section from a rattan walking stick with a fragment of mirror embedded in its handle—useful for peeking around corners without making a target.

More shots were exchanged below, and Bill knew Jane was sunk once she ran out of ammo. His plan was to follow the ridgeline north to a lone cottonwood that sat behind the Lucas boys.

The tricky part was to cover the thirty or so open yards between the ridge and the tree. Bill decided to run, for a low crawl would take too long and increase his chance of being spotted.

He put on a burst of speed. But halfway to the tree, Jip turned around, spotted him, and sang out. Bill ran the last fifteen yards in a humming, whiffing hail of hammering gunfire. One slug passed under his left armpit and tugged his shirt sharply. But he dove safely behind the tree.

Fist-sized hunks of gnarled bark flew from the tree as the Lucas boys tossed lead at him. Bill put his back to the tree. Then, mirror aiming with the cane, he began throwing lead back.

When Olney's flap hat went flying, wiped right off his head, the brothers gave up and fled to their horses, tethered downridge. Bill was tempted to plug their mounts, but checked himself. He had shot horses deliberately before, but only as a last resort. *They*, at least, were innocent. Why reduce himself to the level of pond scum like the Lucas boys?

"Dadgarnit, Bill!" Jane shouted to him. "Look

what them sons of whores did to my Ignatius! I'll rip out their hearts and feed 'em to their assholes, them puke pails!"

Bill reached her position. Huge tears had welled in Jane's bloodshot eyes. She's a lonely woman, Bill thought, and that camel meant the world to her.

"You all right?" he asked, looking for wounds on her.

"Thanks to you, good-lookin'. Looks like *you* done the rescuin' today."

"Get your rig and gear," Bill told her. "I'll take you back, and we'll get you a good horse. Matter fact, I'll ask Matt if you can keep Otis Jones's little ginger. Fine animal."

As they trudged back to Bill's horse, Jane lugging her saddle on one shoulder, she said slyly, "You see what I been telling you? How destiny keeps tossin' you and me together, Billy? When you gonna accept your fate and get hitched up with me?"

At that alarming idea, a shudder moved down Bill's spine.

"Jane," Bill replied stoically, "me and marriage mix like cats and dogs. I ain't much for this 'destiny' business. But I will admit, it *does* appear that you're my cross to bear."

That remarked scorched Jane, and sparks flew from her eyes. "Bill Hickok, you're too wicked to be pitied! Fornicating with that scrawny Jezzie and talking about the cross! Shame on you!"

"Me? Huh! I spoze all your interest in Joshua is

for his soul? Is that why you strip in front of him and offer to 'wind his clock' for him?"

"Aww, horse apples! *He's* just a snack, Bill." Her eyes swept his entire form. "Me, I'm more a meat-and-potatoes gal."

Such talk, and the lust burning in her eyes, made Wild Bill sweat. As they reached his horse, however, an idea occurred to him.

He took a good look at this stout, homely, foul-smelling woman. Face it, he told himself. She's got enough guts to fill a smokehouse. She's also the best female shootist in America—with one possible exception, this little slip of a girl named Annie Oakley. Jane was also leather tough, a good rider, and an excellent tracker.

"Jane," Bill said on a sudden impulse. "What say we shoot the whole poke?"

"Hanh?"

"Shoot the whole poke—get it over with quick. Let's team up."

Jane misunderstood, and her homely face was divided by an ear-to-ear smile. Only now did Bill realize the double meaning of his question.

"Uhh—just temporary, I mean," he hastily amended. "Long enough to ride out and put the quietus on these two dry-gulching, back-shooting sons of bitches?"

Jane looked disappointed. But she stuck out her hand, and Bill shook it.

"Deal," she declared. "Let's put at 'em, Bill. Just one request, though."

"What?"

"No quick head shots for these two," Jane stipulated. "I know you like to kill quick and clean. But I want these two buzzards to pay. We're gonna execute 'em by Indian law, not white man's."

Bill nodded. "You and me got our thoughts tied to the same rail. We're going to make sure the punishment fits their crimes."

Chapter Thirteen

Otis Jones's ginger horse took to Jane instantly. That night she and Wild Bill rode out by moonlight, their faces grim and inevitable. Hickok was determined to keep the Lucas brothers from getting the bit in their teeth again. That meant striking them in their sleep.

This had become personal for Calamity Jane, too, and she was sober as a deacon tonight. To stay alert, she employed an old trick she'd learned from teamsters: She smeared tobacco juice inside her eyelids. The mild sting kept her wide awake.

"Here's where they hobbled their mounts while they ambushed you," Wild Bill declared, swinging down from the saddle to squat near the prints. "Their trail heads north."

Jane was silent and brooding, and Bill knew why. Just to their right, down in that sandy wash, lay her dead camel. And even from here, they could hear the muffled rustle of vulture wings. By morning, the bones would be picked clean.

"Those two will play hell trying to find a safe camp out here," Hickok pointed out. "So they'll prob'ly be camped in the open. That means we got to come up on them mighty damn quiet. You got muffles?"

Bill meant rawhide flaps that were tied around a horse's hooves to pad them against such noises as horseshoes clattering on rocks or hard ground.

Jane nodded. "I sneak out of a lot of towns, Bill. I always carry 'em."

"Good. We'll wait until we're closer."

Bill grabbed leather again and the pair moved off at an easy trot, eyes sweeping the distances like lighthouse beacons. Wild Bill was pleasantly surprised by Jane's steady sense of purpose. True, the stink coming off her could curl paint, and she had all the feminine grace of a wagonload of bricks. But she was steady and faithful in a crisis, like those altar lamps that never went out.

"Rein up," Bill said after about an hour's ride.

They both swung down this time. Bill said, "Let me borrow your sash, wouldja?"

"You spot something?" she inquired, understanding immediately what he meant to do with the sash.

"Could be. Let's find out."

Bill tied the sash over his eyes. For the next twenty minutes or so, they waited patiently. By the time Bill unwrapped his eyes, the pupils had opened even more, increasing his night vision by just enough.

"Yep," he told Jane triumphantly. "I see two horses outlined against the sky. Grazing."

"How far ahead?"

"I'd put it at a mile. Let's muffle our horses."

They covered their horses' iron-shod feet before they swung up and over, moving out again.

"Let's see if we can heist their horses first," Bill suggested.

Jane grunted agreement. That act alone, out here in this endless wasteland, would doom these two murdering barn rats. But neither of them planned to leave it at that.

Soon enough, the horses were plainly visible to both riders. Bill was right, they were grazing in sparse grass.

"I see the last of their campfire," Wild Bill announced. Jane was excellent with horses, an expert at "whispering" them gentle. So Bill waited, holding their mounts, while she sneaked forward.

Perhaps ten minutes later she was back, leading both horses by their picket ropes.

"Good animals," she told Bill. "But abused and neglected. Them two cockroaches have scarred their flanks with spurring. And they ain't seen a currycomb since the Lord made Moses."

"Well, they're yours now," Bill told her. "Take them behind us another few hundred yards, then tie them off. I'll wait here. Take ours, too, while you're at it. But hold on a second."

Jane watched Bill dig into a saddle pocket. She

grinned when he removed a stick of dynamite.

"Since they like to play with explosives," Bill told her, "we'll dose 'em with their own medicine."

"But you've got no blasting cap or fuse," Jane pointed out.

"Those glowing embers will be the fuse."

When Jane had removed the horses and returned, Bill said, "I'm going in. Keep your shooter to hand."

"You don't mean to kill 'em quick in their sleep?" Jane said, worried they would die too mercifully.

"Naw. Just give 'em a rude wake-up call."

They both checked their loads in the silver moonlight, and Bill made sure both Peacemakers were loose and ready in the holsters.

He moved in at a crouch, then a low crawl. Now he could see the dark mounds formed by two sleepers rolled up in blankets. When he was perhaps twenty feet from the fire, he rose to his knees.

He gave the dynamite a careful underhand flip. Bill grinned, well satisfied, when it thumped into the middle of the embers, throwing off sparks. He slid his right-hand gun out, then went facedown.

A boom-cracking explosion rocked the ground, and dirt and debris went slapping everywhere.

"Jee-zus God almighty!"

Both Lucas boys, shocked senseless, scrambled out of their burning bedrolls, cursing like stable sergeants.

"My hair's on fire, Olney!" Jip roared out.

"Hell with that! Bust caps, damnit!"

"Let 'er rip, Jane!" Bill shouted before the two disoriented, burned men could put up any defense.

Deliberately pulling their aim, he and Calamity Jane each tossed in five or six shots. Their gun muzzles spat orange streaks in the darkness.

"Lissenup, this is Hickok! You two are surrounded! You can surrender or die now! What'll it be?"

Given the circumstances, this was no choice at all.

"We'll surrender!" Olney shouted back.

Bill knew damn well what Olney was thinking: They were still a long way from any law, so chances to escape might crop up. Besides, even if they went to prison, prisons could be escaped. But it'll never come to that, he thought as he moved cautiously in.

"Well, now, lookit here," said the cocky Olney as Bill gathered up their firearms. "I finally get to meet Wild Bill Hickok. And who is this lovely— *unh!*"

Calamity Jane smashed him full in the mouth with the twelve-inch barrel of her Smith & Wesson, wiping out his front teeth.

"*You* ain't in control no more, you human cesspool," she snarled at him. "We're the big nabobs here. Next time you insult me, I'll lop off your ball sac!"

With both prisoners securely tied, Jane went back to the horses and returned with a small entrenching tool she had borrowed from Matt.

Olney, his words distorted and garbled now, demanded: "The hell's that for?"

"We're gonna plant a little garden out here," Bill explained in a pleasant voice. "What you might call an ant garden."

"Over here, Bill," Jane called out. "I found some anthills. Red ants."

"Wuh—what the hell you doing?" Olney demanded. "We surrendered."

"We all make mistakes," Bill goaded him. "Like your mistake in killing Otis Jones and Jane's camel and my horse. The biggest damn mistakes you boys ever made. Now you're going to die the way you deserve."

"This—this is vigilante law!" Olney protested. "Why, it's agin' the Constitution."

"God's law prevails out here," Jane assured him. "As ye reap, you murdering sons of bitches, so shall ye sew."

False dawn was lightening the sky by the time their work was finished. Both prisoners were buried up to their necks in anthills. Furious red ants swarmed their heads, so thick no skin was visible. To make sure they couldn't close their eyes against it, Jane had sliced off their eyelids.

As Bill and Jane rode out, the horrific screams behind them did not move either to pity. There was a larger motive in all of this. Wild Bill knew Josh and other writers would report it widely. It was important that criminals out west knew there was swift, harsh justice when other law wasn't available.

By the time they both returned to camp, the sun was blazing. The two "vigilantes" felt tired from their eyes to their insteps. But one last detail remained before the book was finally closed on the Lucas brothers.

Later that day, Calamity Jane returned to lift the scalps of the two men, whose heads, by then, were reduced to raw, shiny skullbone. And "lift" is literally all it required—the hair was no longer attached to anything.

Bill tucked both scalps into a big deerskin pouch. When the Chisholm Trail passed the town of Antelope Wells, Hickok sent the pouch by express messenger to Harding Ott in Ogallala.

"Just to let him know," Bill assured Matt and Joshua, "that we're on our way with a herd of cattle and by God we mean to get there with 'em."

Chapter Fourteen

About two weeks after Wild Bill and Calamity Jane sent the Lucas boys under, Bobcat visited Chinook at the latter's cabin.

As was the custom, there could be no serious conversation until they smoked to the Four Directions. Chinook took out a chamois pouch filled with strong black tobacco. He filled a clay calumet and both men smoked, speaking only of inconsequential matters.

Then Bobcat set the pipe down between them, signaling that he was ready to speak words that had weight.

"You know," the Reservation Police Chief began, "that Ott has sent word? He wants us to attack the cattle drive."

Chinook nodded. "Do you want me to ride with

you?" inquired the aging warrior. "Is that why you have come? I will."

Bobcat shook his head. "No. I have turned this thing over in my mind many times. Like dogs licking our master's hand, we do this white killer's bidding. Do *you* wish to see our people starve so that a few of us can wear white man's shoes?"

Chinook was a weak man, but not a bad one. He only needed another man to stand up and show him the way.

"No, brother, I do not," he replied. "Nor do I like this plan to attack the Ice Shaman. He saved our people once."

"I have ears for this," Bobcat assured him. "Will you come with me now? Will you join me in returning these"—he slapped the new holster and side arm Ott had given him—"to Ott right now?"

Chinook hesitated, fear tightening his features. "He may kill us," he pointed out.

"So? Name a man who will live forever. We will at least die as Lakota men, not apple Indians—red outside, but white inside."

"As you say," Chinook finally agreed. "I have had a full life, and my good woman has passed before me. We will be together again in the Land of Ghosts."

"Good, brother. Well said. Now catch up your pony and let us ride."

Cold dread lay heavy in their bellies as they rode out. They knew the dying, with Ott, would not be easy. He would not kill them today. He would send the Lucas brothers to do it, and they enjoyed a slow killing. But pride and honor pushed both braves all the way.

As they were ground-hitching their horses outside Ott's soddy, Chinook's little paint began to snort and stamp his hooves.

"He has caught the blood smell," Chinook said, glancing warily around them in the rolling green vastness.

The answer lay inside the dreary house. They found the Crow Indian squaw, Woman Dress, lying bruised and battered on her straw pallet, eyes glazed with shock. The interior of the soddy was a shambles.

And Harding Ott lay sprawled before the iron stove, a bone-handle knife buried deep in his heart.

Both braves quickly averted their eyes—the souls of the evil dead could enter a man through his eyes. Both also made slashing movements with their right hand, the cutoff sign for the dead.

Woman Dress was unresponsive at first, but neither brave needed a shaman to assemble this familiar story. Ott's crockery liquor jug, empty, sat beside two scalps on the table. Towhead scalps easily recognizable as those of Jip and Olney Lucas. Clearly, Ott had flown into a rage and beat his woman—one time too many.

"You are the police chief," Chinook told Bobcat. "Will she be turned over to the white man's court or the Lakota headmen?"

"I think neither," Bobcat replied. He looked at the woman. "Did he mean to kill you?"

It was common practice for Indians to beat their wives. Indeed, Bobcat had beaten his own woman only yesterday for failing to repair his moccasins. But unlike the brutal Comanches to the south, the Sioux law-ways did not permit killing a woman except for extraordinary cause such as unfaithfulness.

"Did he mean to kill you, woman?" he demanded again.

"He meant to cut out my child, too," she managed in English. "Kill both of us."

"You swear it in front of the High Holy Ones?" She nodded.

"There is no crime here," Bobcat concluded, satisfied. "We will take his body and bury it where no one can find it."

He looked at the pregnant woman again. "You have no place to go. This home and everything in it is yours. You will stay here and we will send you provisions. When your time comes, our women will help you with the birth."

She nodded, mustering a little smile of gratitude. In that moment, none of the Indians could appreciate the irony of a curious sandalwood carving on the wall above Ott's dead body. It depicted an image of Ganesh, the Hindu god of success—the only god Ott had ever believed in.

One week after the Sioux buried Ott in a secret, unmarked grave, Hickok's Misfits splashed across the "mile-wide but inch-deep" South Platte to great fanfare.

165

A bevy of derby-hatted photographers had set up their cameras. All the exploding flashes spooked the cattle, but it didn't matter now. They scattered out on the lush grass of the reservation and promptly began grazing.

Wild Bill magnanimously insisted that Calamity Jane must pose beside him. And he told every reporter assembled that *she* was the real heroine of this expedition.

Good news awaited them. Ott was gone, and thanks to Indian informants, his Commerce Bluffs scheme had been exposed. The Indian Bureau had already seized his ill-gotten assets and placed them in a trust for the entire Sioux tribe, foreign investors be damned.

Already, Chinook reported, the reservation water holes were safe again. And with Ott and his thugs out of the picture, supplies were slowly getting through again.

Wild Bill, a great favorite with the U.S. Army, recommended medals and promotions for every soldier in the detail. He even surprised young Joshua by telling all the assembled reporters that "your colleague from the *New York Herald* is a damn fine cowboy for a city slicker."

"We friends again, Bill?" the delighted kid demanded.

"We never stopped being friends, Longfellow. But now I ain't tempted to put a boot up your ass."

As for Felicity Parker—she had stuck with the drive to the end. Totally enamored of Wild Bill by now, she had never once even tried to kill him, despite the huge payoff promised her for doing so.

That night, as everyone celebrated at government expense at a saloon in Ogallala, Fel took Bill aside and confessed that she had been Ott's accomplice.

"Hell, I figured as much," Hickok admitted with calm good cheer. "How's come you didn't plug me and collect?"

Her nutshell eyes sparkled with feeling. She took the alligator jewel case out of her reticule and removed the gun.

"This is why," she told him. "It was your complete trust in me, Bill. Everyone calls you such a cynical survivalist who only looks after number one. But you gave me my loaded gun back."

A little grin twitched at his lips as Wild Bill took the derringer from her, cocked it, and held it to his head.

Fel paled. "Bill! My God, what are you—?"

Hickok pulled the trigger, producing only a metallic click. Then he fished into his fob pocket and pulled out the gun's firing pin!

"Trust everyone," he told the wide-eyed, still-shocked beauty, "but *always* cut the cards."

CHEYENNE

Double Edition:
Pathfinder/ Buffalo Hiders
JUDD COLE

Pathfinder. Touch the Sky never forgot the kindness of the settlers, and tried to help them whenever possible. But an old friend's request to negotiate a treaty between the Cheyenne and gold miners brings the young brave face-to-face with a cunning warrior. If Touch the Sky can't defeat his new enemy, the territory will never again be safe for pioneers.
And in the same action-packed volume...
Buffalo Hiders. Once, mighty herds of buffalo provided the Cheyenne with food, clothing and skins for shelter. Then the white hunters appeared and the slaughter began. Still, few herds remain, and Touch the Sky swears he will protect them. But two hundred veteran mountain men and Indian killers are bent on wiping out the remaining buffalo—and anyone who stands in their way.

___4413-7 $4.99 US/$5.99 CAN

Dorchester Publishing Co., Inc.
P.O. Box 6640
Wayne, PA 19087-8640

Please add $1.75 for shipping and handling for the first book and $.50 for each book thereafter. NY, NYC, and PA residents, please add appropriate sales tax. No cash, stamps, or C.O.D.s. All orders shipped within 6 weeks via postal service book rate. Canadian orders require $2.00 extra postage and must be paid in U.S. dollars through a U.S. banking facility.

Name_____
Address_____
City_____ State_____ Zip_____
I have enclosed $_____ in payment for the checked book(s).
Payment <u>must</u> accompany all orders. ❑ Please send a free catalog.
CHECK OUT OUR WEBSITE! www.dorchesterpub.com

CHEYENNE
Spirit Path
Mankiller
Judd Cole

Spirit Path. The mighty Cheyenne trust their tribe's shaman to protect them against great sickness and bloody defeat. A rival accuses Touch the Sky of bad medicine, and if he can't prove the claim false, he'll come to a brutal end.

And in the same action-packed volume . . .

Mankiller. A fierce warrior, Touch the Sky can outfight, outwit, and outlast any enemy. Yet the fearsome Cherokee brave named Mankiller can snap a man's neck as easily as a reed, and he is determined to count coup on Touch the Sky.

___4445-5 $4.99 US/$5.99 CAN

CHEYENNE

GIANT EDITION:

BLOOD ON THE ARROWS

JUDD COLE

Born the son of a Cheyenne warrior, raised by frontier settlers, Touch the Sky returns to his tribe and learns the ways of a mighty shaman. Then the young brave's most hated foe is brutally slain, and he stands accused of the crime. If he can't prove his innocence, he'll face the wrath of his entire people—and the hatred of the woman he loves.
___4734-9 $5.50 US/$6.50 CAN

WILD BILL
DEAD MAN'S HAND
JUDD COLE

Marshal, gunfighter, stage driver, and scout, Wild Bill Hickok has a legend as big and untamed as the West itself. No man is as good with a gun as Wild Bill, and few men use one as often. From Abilene to Deadwood, his name is known by all—and feared by many. That's why he is hired by Allan Pinkerton's new detective agency to protect an eccentric inventor on a train ride through the worst badlands of the West. With hired thugs out to kill him and angry Sioux out for his scalp, Bill knows he has his work cut out for him. But even if he survives that, he has a still worse danger to face— a jealous Calamity Jane.

___4487-0 $3.99 US/$4.99 CAN

WILD BILL

JUDD COLE

THE KINKAID COUNTY WAR

Wild Bill Hickok is a legend in his own lifetime. Wherever he goes his reputation with a gun precedes him—along with an open bounty of $10,000 for his arrest. But Wild Bill is working for the law when he goes to Kinkaid County, Wyoming. Hundreds of prime longhorn cattle have been poisoned, and Bill is sent by the Pinkerton Agency to get to the bottom of it. He doesn't expect to land smack dab in the middle of an all-out range war, but that's exactly what happens. With the powerful Cattleman's Association on one side and land-grant settlers on the other, Wild Bill knows that before this is over he'll be testing his gun skills to the limit if he hopes to get out alive.

WILD BILL

JUDD COLE

BLEEDING KANSAS

Even among the toughest hardcases in the West, Abilene, Kansas, is known as pure hell on earth, a wide-open wild town that was reined in only briefly—when Wild Bill Hickok was its sheriff. Ever since he rode out of Abilene, Wild Bill never wanted to go back. But now he has to. A lot of people are dying fast there. The Kansas Pacific Railroad is laying track where somebody obviously doesn't want it, and bullets are flying thick and furious. The Pinkerton Agency needs their best operative to get to the bottom of it, and that means only one man—Wild Bill. But as hard as it is for Wild Bill to go back, he knows there is a bigger challenge ahead of him—staying alive once he gets there.

___4584-2 $3.99 US/$4.99 CAN

Dorchester Publishing Co., Inc.
P.O. Box 6640
Wayne, PA 19087-8640

WILD BILL

YUMA BUSTOUT

JUDD COLE

When the Danford Gang terrorized Arizona, no one—not the U.S. Marshals or the Army—could bring them in. It took Wild Bill Hickok to do that. Only Wild Bill was able to put them in the Yuma Territorial Prison, where they belonged. But the prison can't hold them. The venomous gang escapes and takes the Governor's wife and her sister as hostages. So it is up to Wild Bill to track them down and do the impossible—capture the Danford Gang a second time. Only this time, the gang's ruthless leader, Fargo Danford, has a burning need for revenge against the one man who put him and the gang in prison in the first place, a need as deadly as the desert trap he has set for Bill.

___4674-1 $3.99 US/$4.99 CAN